PRAISE FOR THE DRAMA HIGH SERIES

"You'll definitely feel for Jayd Jackson, the bold sixteen-year-old Compton, California, junior at the center of keep-it-real Drama High stories."—*Essence* magazine on *Drama High: Jayd's Legacy*

"Egged with comedy and a provoking street-savvy plot line, Compton native and Drama High author L. Divine writes a fascinating story capturing the voice of young black America." —*The Cincinnati Herald* on the Drama High series

"Filled with all the elements that make for a good book— young love, non-stop drama, and a taste of the supernatural, it is sure to please."—The RAWSISTAZ Reviewers on *Drama High: The Fight*

"A captivating look at teen life."—Harriet Klausner on *Drama High: The Fight*

"If you grew up on a steady diet of saccharine-*Sweet Valley* novels and think there aren't enough books specifically for African-American teens, you're in luck."—*The Prince George's Sentinel* on *Drama High: The Fight*

"Through a healthy mix of book smarts, life experiences, and down-to-earth flavor, L. Divine has crafted a well-nuanced coming-of-age tale for African-American youth." —*The Atlanta Voice* on *Drama High: The Fight*

"Drama High has it all . . . fun, fast, addictive."—Cara Lockwood, bestselling author of *Moby Clique*

Published by Kensington Publishing Corporation

DRAMA *HIGH:*
COURTIN' JAYD

A NOVEL

L. Divine

Dafina KTeen Books
KENSINGTON PUBLISHING CORP.
http://www.kensingtonbooks.com

To my publicist at Kensington, Adeola Saul, for having faith in the series and for being an enthusiastic passenger on this journey. From the beginning you've been a consistent cheerleader. Thank you for your continued support.

To Walter, Steven, John, Laurie, Magee, Jessica, Lydia, Barbara, David, Darla, Helen, Selena, and the rest of the folks at Kensington Publishing Corp.: Thank you for being flexible and patient always. To my former publicists, Christal Jordan-Mims in Atlanta and Parthenia Bozeman in Los Angeles, for backing the series from the start.

And to my agent, Brendan Deneen: Thank you for helping to make my dreams a reality and for courting Jayd like a true gentleman.

THE CREW

Jayd

A sassy sixteen-year-old from Compton, California, who comes from a long line of Louisiana conjure women. She is the only one in her lineage born with brown eyes and a caul. Her grandmother appropriately named her "Jayd," which is also the name her grandmother took on in her days as a Voodoo queen in New Orleans. She lives with her grandparents, four uncles, and her cousin Jay. Jayd is in all AP classes and visits her mother on the weekend. She has a tense relationship with her father, whom she sees occasionally, and has never-ending drama in her life, whether at school or home.

Mama/Lynn Mae

When Jayd gets in over her head, her grandmother, Mama, is always there to help her. A full-time conjure woman with magical green eyes and a long list of both clients and haters, Mama also serves as Jayd's teacher, confidante, and protector.

Mom/Lynn Marie

At thirty-something years old, Lynn Marie would never be mistaken for a mother of a teenager. But Jayd's mom is definitely all that and with her green eyes, she keeps the men guessing. Able to talk to Jayd telepathically, Lynn Marie is always there when Jayd needs her.

Esmeralda

Mama's nemesis and Jayd's nightmare, this next-door neighbor is anything but friendly. She relocated to Compton from Louisiana around the same time Mama did and has been a thorn in Mama's side ever since. She continuously causes trouble for Mama and Jayd, interfering with Jayd's school life through Misty, Mrs. Bennett, and Jeremy's mom. Esmeralda's

cold blue eyes have powers of their own, although not nearly
as powerful as Mama's.

Rah

Rah is Jayd's first love from Junior High school who has come
back into her life when a mutual friend, Nigel, transfers from
Rah's high school (Westingle) to South Bay. He knows everything about her and is her spiritual confidant. Rah lives in
Los Angeles but grew up with his grandparents in Compton
like Jayd. He loves Jayd fiercely but has a girlfriend that refuses
to go away (Trish) and a baby-mama (Sandy). Rah is a hustler
by necessity and a music producer by talent. He takes care of
his younger brother Kamal and holds the house down while
his dad is locked up and his mother strips at a local club.

Misty

The word "frenemies" was coined for this former best friend
of Jayd's. Misty has made it her mission to sabotage Jayd any
way she can. Living around the corner from Jayd, she has the
unique advantage of being an original hater from the neighborhood and at school.

KJ

He's the most popular basketball player on campus, Jayd's
ex-boyfriend, and Misty's current boyfriend. Ever since he
and Jayd broke up, he's made it his personal mission to per-
secute her.

Nellie

One of Jayd's best friends, Nellie is the prissy princess of the
crew. She is also dating Chance, even though it's Nigel she's
really feeling. Nellie made history at South Bay by becoming
the first Black Homecoming princess and has let the crown
go to her head.

Mickey

The gangster girl of Jayd's small crew. She and Nellie are best friends but often at odds with each other, mostly because Nellie secretly wishes she could be more like Mickey. A true hood girl, she loves being from Compton and her man with no name is a true gangster.

Jeremy

A first for Jayd, Jeremy is her white ex-boyfriend who also happens to be the most popular cat at South Bay. Rich, tall and extremely handsome, Jeremy's witty personality and good conversation keep Jayd on her toes and give Rah a run for his money—literally.

Mickey's Man

Never using his name, Mickey's original boyfriend is a troublemaker and always hot on Mickey's trail. Always in and out of jail, Mickey's man is notorious in her hood for being a cold-hearted gangster, and loves to be in control. He also has a thing for Jayd but Jayd can't stand to be anywhere near him.

Nigel

The new quarterback on the block, Nigel is a friend of Jayd's from junior high and also Rah's best friend, making Jayd's world even smaller at South Bay High. Nigel is the star football player and dumped his ex-girlfriend at Westingle (Tasha) to be with his new baby-mama to be, Mickey. Jayd is caught up in the mix as both of their friends, but her loyalty lies with Nigel because she's known him longer and he's always had her back.

Chance

The rich white hip-hop kid of the crew, Chance is Jayd's drama homie and Nellie's boyfriend, if you let him tell it. He used to have a crush on Jayd and now has turned his attention to Nellie.

Bryan

The youngest of Mama's children and Jayd's favorite uncle, Bryan is a dj by night and works at the local grocery store during the day. He's also an acquaintance of both Rah and KJ from playing ball around the hood. Bryan often gives Jayd helpful advice about her problems with boys and hating girls alike. Out of all of Jayd's uncles, Bryan gives her grandparents the least amount of trouble.

Jay

Jay is more like an older brother to Jayd than her cousin. Like Jayd, he lives with Mama but his mother (Mama's youngest daughter) left him when he was a baby and never returned. He doesn't know his father and attends Compton High. He and Jayd often cook together and help Mama around the house.

Prologue

"*Haven't you heard of no white after Labor Day, Jayd?*" *Mrs. Bennett, my most hated teacher, says, commenting on my bright attire. Apparently, it's okay for folks to wear all black on any given day. But put on white from head to toe, and you stick out like a sore thumb.*

"*Other people's opinions of you don't matter, Jayd. It's what you think of yourself and your heritage that counts,*" *Mama says, creeping into my dream as usual. Do all grandmothers have this ability, or is it just mine?*

"*She's right, Jayd,*" *my mom says. I guess my dream world has become community property.* "*I know it's difficult sticking out in a crowd, especially at school, but it's worth it. Trust me.*" *And I know she knows what she's talking about. My mom gave up on her spirit lessons in high school. So why are they all up in my head this morning?*

"*Look at that witch,*" *Reid says, no longer in character as Macbeth but joined by the rest of the drama class in his taunting.* "*My mom told me about people like you.*"

"*Yeah, my great grandmother remembered hearing stories about slaves with strange powers,*" *Mrs. Bennett says. What is she doing in drama class? She and Mrs. Sinclair don't get along at all.* "*They had to be put in their place to protect the others on the plantation," she says, raising her pointer above her head, which she yields like a weapon in class on a regular basis, ready to strike.*

"Fight back, Jayd, like I taught you to," Mama whispers into my ear as I stand my ground in the center of the room. Everyone has surrounded me, ready to watch the whipping I'm supposed to receive. "None of our ancestors took shit laying down, Jayd. We come from a long line of warriors. Girl, get up and fight!"

"You have no right to judge me," I say, taking a step back from Mrs. Bennett. None of my friends are here to help me. Only my enemies have come to watch. "And you damn sure have no right to hit me," I say. Mrs. Bennett looks at me, her cold blue eyes shimmering like our wicked neighbor Esmeralda's did when she gave me my headache from hell, which starts again as I stare back at her. What the hell?

I feel like Alice in Wonderland. Watching me stumble and fall to my knees in the center of the circle, the entire class laughs hysterically at my demise. At any minute I'm going to vomit from the dizziness in my head. The laughing is getting louder and more dramatic. The scene switches and Reid is now in character. But instead of being Lady Macbeth, I'm one of the witches. Alia's still laughing along with the rest of the onlookers as Mrs. Bennett readies herself to take a cheap shot at me while I'm already down.

"Jayd, don't you hear that alarm, girl? Get up," Mama yells from her bed, instinctively saving me from my psychic beatdown.

"Sorry, Mama. I'm off my game a little this morning," I say, shaking my head free of the leftover pounding from my dream. I haven't seen Esmeralda since I gave Misty her gris-gris ingredients last week and I leave out of the back door now always, just in case she's feeling bold. After getting a taste of her powers, I'll never give Esmeralda the chance to catch me off-guard again.

"As soon as you realize It's a game you can master, you won't ever be off it again," Mama says, giving me insight into my own visions, as usual. How does she do that?

"She's Mama," my mom says, contributing her two cents. "You haven't even seen ten percent of what she can really do. Why do you think I stay out of her way?"

"If your mom's in your head, please tell her to call me. It's time for her to get a reading about this new man of hers," Mama says, rolling over in her bed and returning to sleep. When did I become a psychic mailwoman?

"Mama says to call her," I say out loud, knowing they both heard me.

"Damn, see what I mean Jayd? She probably already did the reading and wants to see what I have to say. Ain't no hiding from Mama." And don't I know it. I'll have to talk to her about my dream later. Now it's time to get to school and face the music. Things have been really tense since everyone found out about me trying to help Misty, especially when I came to school wearing all white last week. But, I'm not going to be deterred from living my life. And with my crew back together as tight as glue, I know I'll be just fine.

~ 1 ~
Above The Rim

*"The world is mine when I wake up/
I don't need nobody telling me the time."*

—ERYKAH BADU

From my dream this morning, I thought my day was going to be much more eventful than it was. It was chill though, just going to my classes and getting my assignments for the week. Mrs. Malone still hasn't returned my paper to me. I'm anxious to see what I got on the rewrite. It was a difficult assignment and I wasn't into it at all. I hope there will be fewer red marks across the pages when I get it back this time.

I did notice people staring at me, but it wasn't as bad as I thought it was going to be. And me looking extra flyy today gives them a different impression than the one they had of me last week, even though I look flyy in my whites too.

"Jayd, wait up," Nellie says, joining me as I head toward the gymnasium. While I have dance class, she, Mickey, and the rest of the South Central kids have P.E. during sixth period. I usually don't see any of them walk in because I'm always late for dress-up. Hiking up the hill from drama class is no joke and takes up the majority of the six minutes we have to get from one class to the other, no matter how far apart the classes are. Luckily, we have ten minutes to dress, which gives me plenty of time to get ready and be on time for roll call.

"Why aren't you in the gym already?" I say, speed walking up the steep hill. Students are rushing in every direction before the final bell for sixth period rings. "Don't you have to run laps if you aren't there for roll?" Regular P.E. is more stringent than our elective courses on the AP track, and I always hear about the tougher rules from both her and Mickey. They think I've got it easier because I seemingly have more options, but, like the saying goes, you can't judge a book by its cover.

"Yeah, but we have a sub today," she says and instantly I know it's Mr. Adewale, the fine-ass sub who's been working here for the past couple of weeks. Damn, I wish I had her class today. "And check it out. Nigel, Chance, and Jeremy are playing a game of basketball against KJ and his boys. You've got to come watch."

"What the hell are they doing that for?" I say, obviously more out of the loop than I realized. I missed kicking it with them at lunch because I was rehearsing in drama class, and nothing seemed unusual at break.

"Because they're boys," Nellie says, pulling me in the direction of the main gymnasium instead of to the back area where the dance studio, Olympic-sized pool, and weight rooms are housed. I have a good view of the football field from my class, but the outside basketball courts are on the other side of the building, which is where all sparring matches are held, unless it's raining, like it's supposed to do this afternoon.

"Yeah, but don't they have football practice now?" Chance and Jeremy are seniors and elected not to have classes the last period of the day, especially since they aren't athletes. They'd usually be at the beach right about now. It's mid-November and getting cooler, making surfing uncomfortable I suppose. But still, a game against KJ is tantamount to suicide and I can't imagine the fun in that.

"Yeah, but Mr. Donald had a meeting, so the team just has to run drills and lift weights today. But, they all got into it in fourth period today, arguing about some stupid shit," Nellie says, shaking her head at the painful memory. "KJ challenged Nigel to a game of one-on-one and Nigel accepted, but it quickly turned into three-on-three when Del and C Money wanted in on the action. Chance had Nigel's back, making Jeremy an honorary team player, of course."

"Of course," I say. I can't believe two of my exes and Rah's best friend are all about to engage in a basketball game. And I wonder what they were arguing about in the first place. "How did this all start again?"

As I step into the gymnasium, the bell rings loudly above our heads. I see Jeremy, Chance, and Nigel on the opposite side of the courts, practicing their free throws. I know Nigel's jump shot, but I've never seen Jeremy or Chance ball.

"I can't remember exactly, but I know it had something to do with money," she says. I hope it isn't about KJ placing bets on me and Jeremy's break-up. Before I can continue my questioning, Mr. Adewale comes out of the boy's locker room in a blue and gray Adidas warm-up suit. Damn, he looks good, and he's much taller than I remember.

"Hey y'all," Mickey says, entering the gymnasium, tardy as usual. "Have they started yet?"

"Not yet," Nellie says, following my eyes across the court. "Jayd, what are you looking at?"

"My future baby-daddy," I say, amusing my girls. I try to make eye contact with Mr. Adewale, but he's got eyes for his clipboard and whistle only.

"I know you're not talking about that nappy-headed teacher, are you?" Nellie's not into natural hair at all. Whenever I wear my hair in Afro-puffs, she clowns me for a week straight. "Jayd, please tell me you don't like dreads."

"What can I say? I prefer a natural black man, especially after dealing with KJ's pretty behind," I say, watching KJ and his boys strut into the gymnasium. Nigel and his team stop and stare down their opponents. KJ and his team face them on the court, ready to ball. They know they've got this game in the bag. I actually feel sorry for my boys. I hope their egos are strong enough to survive the ass-whipping they're about to receive.

"Come on, let's get a seat," Mickey says. As we walk up the bleachers, the rest of my dance class, my dance teacher, and the other sixth-period activity classes file into the open space. I know they're not here to witness the impromptu ball game.

"Jayd, I see you made it to class after all," Ms. Carter says. She's hella cool and basically lets us make up our own routines. I always dance solo so that I can dance to my own music, unlike the rest of the white girls in the class who practice their ballet steps all period. I use the class to get a good workout to my reggae and hip-hop CDs.

"Yes, Ms. Carter," I say as my girls take a seat in the bleachers. I hope Ms. Carter doesn't make me sit with our class.

"Good. I was just about to hand in my roll sheet and didn't want you to get marked absent. The gym teachers have a meeting right now and I'm leaving you to the sub over there. Make sure he knows you're here," she says, leaving me to chill with my girls and flirt with Mr. Adewale. This day's looking up minute by minute.

"I have to go check in real quick," I say, tossing my backpack down by my girls' feet and jogging back down the bleachers toward Mr. Adewale.

"But Jayd, you're going to miss the game. They're only playing until the end of the period." Nellie's too into this game for me. I get enough of watching brothas ball from my uncles at home. They have a basketball hoop attached to the top of the garage and ball whenever the mood hits them.

"I'll be right back. Besides, we all know who's going to win." Mickey and Nellie both look at me like I'm the biggest traitor alive. I guess since their boyfriends are playing, it's personal for them. And I have to admit, I would love to see Jeremy whip KJ's ass. But I know different. I just hope Jeremy doesn't get humiliated too bad.

"Hello, Miss Jackson," our substitute says as I approach the crowd where my class is standing. My fellow classmates are too busy salivating over him to notice me walk up late. Wait until he's here every day. Ms. Toni's right, I refuse to be one of these girls. But I do like his style. Maybe for now he can be the big brother I never had. "Glad you could make it this afternoon," he says, giving me a sly smile as he erases the absent mark from my name.

"Sorry I'm late. I was in here the whole time," I say, but I know he's just giving me a hard time.

"It's okay. Have a seat with the rest of the class and we'll begin shortly."

"Oh, but Mr. Adewale," I say, looking across the gym at my girls who are completely engrossed in the game while I'm missing crucial moments. "I was hoping I could sit on the other side and watch the basketball game, if it's okay with you." Lord knows I would much rather get to know him better, but I've got to support my boys.

"But your class is over here, Jayd. And your teacher does have a lesson plan for me to follow, which means I'll need all of the students present. But look on the bright side, you don't have to get dressed today," he says, smiling as he continues to call off names from the roll sheet. How do I get him to cut me some slack? It's not that serious, I know.

"Mr. Adewale," I say in my sweetest voice. "Can I please be excused, just this one time? It's a very important game and I've already missed the first five minutes." But Mr. Adewale isn't budging. Now what?

"Use your eyes, girl. Those pretty brown things are for more than seeing with," my mom says, creeping into my

thoughts. But this time I'm glad. *"Just try it. Keep staring at him and think of the outcome you want, like Mama taught you. And whatever you do, don't let go of your gaze."*

"Jayd," Mickey shouts from across the packed room. There are a couple of smaller games going on, but most of the students are kicking it in the bleachers, waiting for the period to end. "Get your ass over here girl. We need you." Following my mother's advice, I lock onto Mr. Adewale and I can't help but fixate on his flawless butterscotch skin. Looking unmoved at first, Mr. Adewale continues his duties, seemingly unaffected by my plea. But my eyes are wearing him down and he can't resist my request.

"Fine Jayd. But make sure you practice your drills at home. There will be a quiz tomorrow and you will have to incorporate the drills into your own routine."

"Thank you so much," I say, ready to dart off toward my girls. "And can I call you Mr. A?"

"Not if you expect me to answer," he says, smiling at me as I walk backwards toward my destination.

"Damn, what took you so long? You almost missed the whole thing," Mickey says, munching on her Funions as Nellie preps herself in the mirror.

"Don't you think you're exaggerating a bit? And Nellie, why are you worried about your makeup right now? We're in the gym."

"So what? The Homecoming Princess always represents the court and I must look flyy at all times," she says, closing the small compact and returning it to her purse as Mickey rolls her eyes, trying to ignore our girl. "Besides, Chance will be devastated after KJ finishes with him and I want to put a smile on his face."

"Nellie, sometimes you really make my butt itch, you know that? Homecoming is over," Mickey says, smacking on the tangy chips. They do smell good.

"You should talk, bringing those stank-ass things in here. You know there's no eating in the gym," Nellie says, pointing to the multiple signs posted throughout the room. "I can't believe you're still hungry after that lunch you ate anyway."

"Shut up Nellie and watch the game," Mickey says, a little more serious than necessary. I wonder what's got her panties in a bunch.

"Everything okay Mickey?" I ask, grabbing a Funion out of the near-empty bag. Nellie's right: our girl can eat. "You seem tense today."

"Yes Jayd, I'm fine. I want to watch the rest of the game in peace, if y'all don't mind." No, something's definitely wrong with her. She's being bitchy, even for Mickey.

"Ouch," Nellie says, responding to KJ dunking on Nigel's head. Damn, I know that hurt.

"And that's what we like to call 'above the rim'," Dell says, talking shit to Chance as he guards him. "You see all that air KJ left for y'all?"

"Less talking, more ballin'," Jeremy says, stealing the rebound from C Money and taking the ball back up the court.

"Oh, so the white boy thinks he can ball," KJ says, but even he can't front: he's impressed with Jeremy's skills. "You're not going to beat me on my own court." Talking shit is KJ's second-best sport. It seems to go hand in hand with being a good basketball player.

"We'll see about that," Nigel says, catching Jeremy's pass before shooting for three. "Did you hear the sound of that? That's what we refer to as a swoosh," Nigel says, laughing all the way back up the court.

"Yeah, well this is what we refer to as a tiebreaker," KJ says, dribbling into Jeremy, through Chance, and around Nigel for a perfect layup.

"Foul," Chance says and he's right. But the rules are dif-

ferent in street ball and that's new territory for both him and
Jeremy.

"Dude, you can't step on someone's feet and still take it to
the hoop," Jeremy says, stepping into KJ's face as the warning bell rings. Most of the students have already started to
head out of the gym, waiting for the final bell to ring. My
dance class is still in awe of Mr. A, who's on his way back to
the boy's locker room. And me and my crew are staying
posted, waiting to see if this game will end in bloodshed.

"Dude," KJ says, mocking Jeremy. "There's no referee here,
if you haven't noticed." KJ and Jeremy are the same height
and probably about the same weight. If they fight, it's going
to be an even brawl and I ain't missing a beat, even if I do
miss my bus.

"Yeah, dude. And that's game," Del says, rubbing salt into
their wounds. "Take it like a man."

"I would if you played like one," Nigel says, throwing his
own shit in the mix. "Y'all play worse than the Lakers when
Shaq and Kobe were competing for best bitch of the league."

"Who you calling a bitch?" KJ says, stepping out of Jeremy's
face and into Nigel's. Even if Nigel stands a few inches shorter,
KJ doesn't want to mess with him. Nigel was recruited to sack
players for South Bay and he'd be glad to do it right here on
the basketball court, if need be.

"Is everything alright over here?" Mr. Adewale says, catching us all off-guard. Me and my girls are mesmerized by the
scene, waiting to see who will throw the first blow. And Chance,
Nigel, and Jeremy all look ready for a fight.

"Yeah man, everything's cool," Nigel says, being the first to
back down. "This game isn't over."

"Anytime, any place baby. You call it and I'll be there," KJ
says as he and his team retreat toward the locker room. "It's
going to be my court no matter where we play."

"We'll see about that," Nigel says, passing the ball to Mr. Adewale as he comes to give Mickey a kiss before heading back to the weight room. I hope he works off some of that frustration before he hurts someone.

"Jayd, you want a ride? From the looks of it, it's about to storm," Mickey says, suddenly in a generous mood. There must be some magic in Nigel's lips because my girl's mood has completely changed.

"Yeah, thanks. Chance, are you okay?" I say, noticing the black scuffmarks across his new kicks and I know how sensitive dudes can be about their shoes.

"Yeah, I'm cool. Jeremy, you should've kicked his ass when you had the chance, man."

"That's not the way to handle it, trust me," Mr. Adewale says, dribbling the ball and shooting some practice hoops. I see he's got game, too. "But, you should have a ref around next time, just in case."

"You're right, man. Next time," Jeremy says, responding to Mr. Adewale but looking at me. I think we should hit the road before I get into some trouble of my own.

"I have to get going," I say, signaling my girls to get up. "Good game. I'm impressed with both of you."

"Why thank you, Lady J," Jeremy says as Chance takes Nellie by the hand, escorting her down the bleachers. "You ladies want to grab something to eat?"

"Oh, I can't. I've got a ton of work to do." I wish I could hang out more after school like other students do, but Mama would have my ass in a sling if I didn't stick to my regular schedule. "But how about tomorrow? It's an early day."

"Tomorrow it is," Jeremy says, helping me down too. I forgot how much of a gentleman he can be.

"And thanks for being our cheerleaders," Chance says, kissing Nellie's hand as Mickey leads the way out of the gym. I think she's had enough of us and our white boys for one day.

By the time we get to the parking lot, it's raining heavily and most of the cars are gone.

"Mickey, do you have my sweater in the car?" Nellie asks, getting in the back since I'll be dropped off first.

"No, I left it at home. I'll get it to you tomorrow," Mickey says, starting the car as Keisha Cole and Missy Elliot blare out of her speakers, making the trunk shake.

"No, Mickey. I need it now. I have my outfit picked out for tomorrow and it includes my red Bebe sweater. You'll have to take me to your house to get it."

"Ah, hell no. I've got to get home," I say, emphatic about not going to the other side of Compton today. I'm not in the mood for seeing Mickey's family, her man included. "Besides, that's out of her way to go all the way to her house and then back to mine."

"Not if she takes the 105. And besides, you were supposed to give me back that sweater weeks ago. I'm not getting out of this car until I have it in my hand." Nellie can be more demanding than Mickey sometimes. It's a wonder they're friends at all.

"Fine. I'll give you your damned sweater," Mickey says, barely catching the on-ramp to the 105 East from the 110. I don't feel good about this detour at all. I knew I should've taken the bus home, even if it meant getting a little wet. It's better than dealing with Mickey's side of town any day.

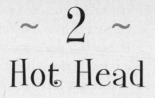

~ 2 ~
Hot Head

*"In and out, out and in you go/
I feel your fire then I lose my self-control."*

—LISA FISCHER

As we approach the Long Beach Boulevard exit, my stomach tightens up and I get the feeling that something's up. It could be paranoia, but I know better. Every time I come to Mickey's house, some shit goes down. If her mama and daddy ain't at each other's throats, then her brothers and sister are tripping. Not to mention that her man is usually in close proximity, which is always a negative experience for me.

"I hate coming to your side of town," Nellie says, expressing my sentiments exactly. "Why couldn't you just bring my sweater to school when I first asked you to?"

"Because I forgot. What's the big deal? You only live five minutes away from here," Mickey says. "And Jayd, doesn't your daddy live over here somewhere?" Mickey intones, recalling my first visit to her crib where I mentioned I was familiar with her hood. Most of my friends from my old school, Family Christian, live out this way, including Rah's grandparents.

"Yeah, he lives by the old Lynwood High." Even though my dad lives directly behind the Compton Swap Meet, his side of town is considered Lynwood and he's very proud of not actually living in the city of Compton, just like Nellie.

"Want to stop by and give him a shout-out?" Mickey says,

making light of the fact me and my dad barely speak. I haven't seen him since we went to a family picnic together a couple of months ago. He called and left a message afterwards but I never did return his call. I'll make sure to give him a call tomorrow. Even if I can't stand the man, he's still my father and my elder, which means I have to respect him, or so he says to me all the time.

"We don't have time for family visits or any other kinds of stops. I need to get home and touch up my hair," Nellie says, tucking a wayward strand behind her ear before silencing her ringing cell.

"Nellie, you act like you live in another county," Mickey says pulling into her driveway where her family's outside kicking it. "You live right up the street from me, same area code and all."

"Yeah, but you live in Compton and I live in Rosewood. Very different energies between the two places," she says, sounding as bougie as ever. I knew Nellie's foul experience with Tania and her crew wouldn't have a permanent effect on the diva in our girl.

"Yeah, whatever. Tell that to the brothas who've pledged their lives to the streets of Compton, right on your block," says Mickey, and she would know. Her younger brothers and her man are in that category. And speaking of which, her man pulls up right behind Mickey's car, blocking us in. This trip isn't going to be as quick as I anticipated.

"Ah damn," Mickey says, turning off the engine and opening the car door. "I was supposed to call him after school and forgot." She didn't forget as much as she was distracted by her other man ballin'. Mickey better tighten her game or she's going to be in more trouble than she can handle.

"How long are you going to keep this juggling act going, Mickey? You know you're playing with fire," I say. I don't mean to sound like her mama, but damn. I'm being put in an

uncomfortable situation no matter how it goes and personally, I'm sick of it.

"I know you're not talking," Mickey says, looking at me
through the rearview mirror before getting out. And she's right.
I'm slightly torn between Jeremy and Rah still. But at least
I'm not playing anyone. The way she's working the game, it
can only end up bad for everyone involved.

"Mickey, where you been? I told you to call me when you
got out of class," her man says, getting out of his car without
even turning it off. Mickey's man is hotter than hot and that
ain't good. Nellie and I watch it all go down as her family
members ignore the dramatic scene. I guess this happens on
a daily basis around here. Mickey's man takes a large step toward her and snatches her by the arm, making her drop the
new cell phone in her hand. I wonder if he knows it was a
gift from Nigel.

"Damn boo, chill," she says, pulling away from him and
going for her phone on the ground. But it's no use. He grabs
her arm again, this time tighter, and pulls her in closer so she
can't get away.

"Who you messing with, Mickey, huh?" he says, smelling
her hair like a dog. What the hell? If a dude ever tried that
shit with me, his days would be numbered. "What's his name?"

"Damn, nigga, calm down. It ain't even like that," Mickey
says, trying to save face. How she keeps her lies straight I'll
never know. "We just got here and I have to run inside and
get something for Nellie before I take my girls home." He
looks inside the car and sees Nellie and me looking dead at
him. I wish I had Esmeralda's eyes right about now. I'd like to
give him a headache from hell like only she can.

"Whatever, Mickey. I know you been screwing somebody
else and I'm going to find out who it is, one way or another.
Get your ass in the house and get whatever it is you need to
get. We'll take your girls home together," he says, pushing

her toward the front door. He sounds more like her daddy than her man. But I guess since her dad's too busy working two jobs to support his extra-large family, her man's the only regular father figure she's got.

"I don't want to ride in the car with him," Nellie says, looking at me with a panicked expression. "And I don't want him knowing where I live. What do we do?" she says, turning around in her seat and digging in her purse for her phone again.

"I don't know what you're going to do, but I'm taking the bus home like I should've done in the first place," I say, taking my bus pass out of my purse and putting it in my jacket pocket. "Now, let me out so I can get my stroll on."

"Jayd, are you serious? You're going to walk around here by yourself and in that red top? Are you crazy?"

"We're in blood territory," I say, zipping up my jacket so as not to attract too much attention to myself. The last thing I need is more drama in my life. "Besides, no one's going to mess with me anyway." Between my notorious grandmother and my infamous uncles, everyone in this city knows my family's not to be messed with. The only people that don't care are my neighborhood haters, but that's because of their loyalty to Misty's trifling behind. Otherwise, they wouldn't bother me either.

"Jayd, in all good conscience, I can't let you out of this car," Nellie says, sitting back firmly in her seat so I can't fold it forward, no matter how hard I push. "You'll be safer with us."

"I'll see you at school tomorrow Nellie," I say, sliding to the driver's side and pushing my way out of the car. Mickey's man comes over to watch me struggle out of the backseat of the classic vehicle. I feel like a little kid trying to climb out of a car seat. My clothes are completely wrinkled and my heavy backpack almost causes me to tumble over, but I catch myself before that happens.

"Going somewhere?" he says with his arms crossed tightly over his chest like an evil genie. He might be able to make Mickey's wishes come true, but I'm not impressed.

"Yeah, home. And before you ask, no I don't need an escort," I say, closing the door behind me and walking back down the short driveway. Mickey's siblings glance my direction and continue what they're doing. Thank goodness the rain stopped or my bus ride home would be even more inconvenient.

"Are you sure you don't want a ride? There's more than enough room for you," he says, licking his lips and giving me a devious smile. I know this fool isn't trying to hit on me with his girlfriend in the house a few feet away. What does Mickey see in him? Yeah, he's tall and he looks okay. But as far as personality goes, he's one of the most unattractive men I've ever seen.

"I got your sweater, girl. Let's go," Mickey says, rushing out of her house and down the porch steps. "What's going on here?" Mickey asks, making her way to the car before I'm completely off her property.

"I'm going home. I'll see you in the morning," I say, not waiting for her response. I'm done with this tired scene, for real. If I never see her man again, it'll be too soon. I feel bad for leaving Nellie alone in their madness but it's her choice. It's not my fault she's too prissy to take the bus.

After walking back to Long Beach Boulevard, I catch the bus to Wilmington and Alondra, which will drop me in front of my regular bus stop by Miracle Market. I settle at the bus stop and call Rah, who—for the second time this afternoon—doesn't answer. What's really going on? I thought we agreed after the last time I didn't return his calls for a few days that we wouldn't put each other through that again. I'm trying to give him the benefit of the doubt, but he sure is making it difficult. I might as well give my dad a call now while I'm thinking about it.

I locate my dad's number in my contact list and press send on my worn-out cell. The last thing I want to do is have a long conversation with him, which usually ends in an argument. I'm going to make this as brief as possible.

"Hello there, youngin'," my dad says, sounding as country as ever. The sound of his voice alone gives me shivers.

"Hey Daddy. I'm just checking in. How are you?" I ask. The bus is down the street and approaching my stop, giving me the perfect reason to cut short our conversation if need be.

"I'm fine, girl. How are you?" He usually sounds happy to hear from me but he feels the same way about chatting with me as I do: less is definitely more.

"I'm fine. Waiting at the bus stop. How's the family?" His side is more like a clan that I'm not a part of, but I'm trying to be sweet like Mama taught me.

"Your stepmama and brother and sister are fine, but you'd know that if you came by more often," he says. What am I supposed to do—fly to his house? He knows I'm dependent on others for a ride and my mom damn sure ain't taking me over there. When she left him before I was born, she swore she'd never step foot in that house again and she hasn't broken her word yet.

"I would come over more often if I had a way there," I say, but we both know that's a lie. I could think of a million other places to go before stopping in his hood. It's enough that I have to attend his family functions. But voluntarily spending time with him isn't an option.

"Well, you never did get back to me about your driving lessons. I already told you I'd pay for them," he says. I can tell from his tone he's salty about me stalling. I'd rather earn the money and pay for them myself than take the offer from him, which will inevitably have a price of its own.

"Right," I say as the bus pulls up. "I've been pretty busy and I'm looking for a new job," I say without telling him I no longer have my job at Simply Wholesome. I don't want to hear his mouth about that one. "But anytime you set it up should be good."

"A new job? What's wrong with the one you have?" he asks, fishing for more information. I've been working since I was ten years old because of his refusal to pay child support properly—he doesn't have the right to question me about my money.

"I need more money." And a better schedule and independence, but he doesn't need to know all that.

"Well, I can respect that," he says. People are lining up to get on the bus and I hate to talk on the phone while I'm riding. "I'll give them a call and let you know when it starts. Should they pick you up from school or your grandmother's house?"

"School would be better for me. My bus is here so I've got to go," I say, rising from my seat and joining the long line of passengers. Some dude is putting a bike on the front of the bus, and that always takes a long time.

"All right then, Jayd. I'll talk to you later. Before you know it, you'll be driving and you won't have to wait at the bus stop anymore." From his lips to God's ears.

"Does that mean you're going to help me buy a car?" I ask, sounding hopeful even though I should know better. My daddy offering to help is a miracle all by itself. I really shouldn't push it.

"I'll pay for the lessons. You and your mother will have to work out the rest," he says, deflating my bubble before it gets full. Why do I even bother?

"What's the point of having a license if I have nothing to drive? And, how is my mom supposed to help me when she barely makes enough for us to live on?" Or did he forget he left her with nothing and pays no alimony?

"I'm sure some of her men will help out," he says. My dad

is always salty about my mom's independence. Honestly, I can't see how they ever got together. They're so different and he's a control freak to the max. But rather then sass him, I hold my tongue and rush him off the phone.

"Dad, I'm losing my signal," I say, walking up the steps to show the driver my pass. She glances at it and shakes her head at me for being on the phone, pointing to the multiple signs that say "No cell use." She doesn't have to tell me twice.

"Be safe and I'll talk to you later," he says before hanging up the phone. I wonder if he treats my sister the same way he treats me. I also wonder how his new wife tolerates his behavior. Maybe she doesn't mind and, I admit, he does have his good points, but he rarely lets me see them.

When I get home, I'll start on my homework for the week and do a little studying in the spirit book if I have time. I never did find the tea my mother listed in her notebook to stop Esmeralda nor did I make the gris-gris for Rah to keep the broads away from him. I want to ask her about the tea this weekend when I see her and talk to her and Mama about my dad paying for my driving lessons. If anything gets both of their heads hot, it's the subject of my father. I'll wait until I'm at Netta's shop tomorrow to break the news to Mama. At least there I'll have some backup, in case Mama explodes.

Ever since yesterday's scene with Mickey's man, I've been avoiding Mickey like the plague, which also meant avoiding kicking it with Jeremy and the rest of the crew all day long. All I wanted to do was to be by myself and study. And it doesn't help that I have to see Reid and Laura at lunch rehearsals and in class every day. I must admit, Reid is good at his role as Macbeth but that still doesn't change the fact that he's an ass. I haven't missed being in a room with him, but he seems to be enjoying our unplanned reunion. He always goaded me into arguments last year when we were on the debate team together. But I've had enough of Reid for one lifetime.

I've been anxious about talking to Netta all day. I know she prefers to work alone, but I hope she lets me be her apprentice. Netta's hair skills are tight and she could also use the company. Before I have a chance to talk to her about it, she and Mama attack me as I walk in the door, and they've been grilling me the entire afternoon since. I knew I shouldn't have told my mom about my dad's offer last night when she probed my mind. She can't keep a secret for nothing.

"Jayd, you really should think twice about letting your daddy pay for your lessons. Girl, you know how manipulative he can be," Netta says, clamping the hot curlers fresh out of the miniature oven sitting at her station. "Tell her, Lynn Mae. Tell that girl how manipulative her daddy can be."

"Calm down, Netta, before you burn my ears," Mama says, folding down her right ear so Netta can curl her hair. I'm always amazed at how quickly Mama's hair grows. "Jayd knows who she's dealing with."

"But it's like making a deal with the devil, Lynn Mae. Tell her." I think Netta's more passionate about hating my daddy than Mama is.

"Okay, to be fair I think he's just trying to help in his own way," I say. Usually I wouldn't dare defend my daddy, especially not to them. But they're missing the bigger picture, which is to my advantage ultimately: I get to learn how to drive and that's more important than their vendetta.

"Help, my ass, Jayd," Mama says, spinning herself around to face me. "I know you know better than that. You just want the same thing your mother wanted: a car. And like your mama, you'll settle to get it." Damn, it's like that? If I let my daddy help me, I'm settling? I just want something that normal teenagers have.

"Mark your grandmother's words, Jayd," Netta says, tilting Mama's head forward to put the final touches on her crown. "That man don't mean you no good. I hate to talk to you like that about your daddy, but it's the truth or this ain't Netta's Never Nappy Beauty Shop," she says, waving the hot curlers toward the neon sign on the front window.

"She's right, Jayd. Your daddy has a history of hurting your mother through you. Don't give him another chance." I know Mama's right. His little comment about my mother's men wasn't a slipup. He knows he's got something I want and will find a way to use it to his advantage. Mama sure knows how to make me feel like a traitor, but I don't see them offering me an alternative to what my main goal is: vehicular independence. And I think this is the perfect time to bring up my job proposal.

"Well, I could pay for the lessons myself if I had a source of steady income," I say, getting up from my seat at the dryers and walking over to Netta's stool. I think I'll have more influence if I hug her up a little bit.

"Uh oh, I smell a plot," Mama says as Netta sprays oil sheen all over Mama's hair, creating a sweet-smelling mist in the air. She and Mama make the best hair products.

"Not a plot, a proposal," I say, handing Netta the plan I typed up this morning at break. "I want to work here part-time, Fridays to start and Saturdays once I get my own wheels. I can be your apprentice," I say, putting my arm around her shoulders as she looks over my work.

"Jayd, how is working here one day a week going to help you get your license?" Mama says. I expected some opposition from her, especially since I've been slacking in my spirit work. But she knows I need a job and this is the best place for me to perfect my braiding skills.

"Well, as the plan outlines in detail . . ." I say, ready to make my case. I've been practicing my speech for days: "If I start out at seven dollars an hour working ten hours a week, plus tips, I'll be able to save enough for a nice down payment on a car, and insurance, by my birthday."

"Jayd, I've always worked alone," Netta says, putting down my paper before taking Mama's robe off. "But I could use some help around here. I'll think about it." Yes. That's all I needed to hear. I know her and Mama will go back and forth about it for a couple of days. But with Netta on my side, I know I can make this work. I may not need my father's help after all and I know that'll be a big plus for Mama. For now, I'll just have to wait and see what happens. I can't wait to tell Rah the good news.

~ 3 ~
Waiting

"How long has it been/
It seems like a mighty long time."

—BARBARA LEWIS

Mama and I hardly spoke a word to each other when we walked home yesterday afternoon. I hope she lets me work with Netta, if Netta decides to hire me. My final paycheck from Simply Wholesome should be at my mom's house when I get there on Friday, but that's two days away and a sistah's broke now. Luckily I don't have to worry about lunch for the next few weeks while we're rehearsing for the play. But after that I'm going to be eating bananas all day until I can get some steady money flowing in.

Speaking of money, I wonder if my Uncle Bryan will let me borrow some cash to tide me over until I get my check, if need be. He's been in such a generous mood lately and it wouldn't hurt to ask.

"I don't know if I feel comfortable letting you borrow money from me without a job, Jayd. That's bad business," Bryan says while he picks his Afro in the mirror. It's bad enough I didn't make it to the bathroom before him this morning. Now I have to hear his perpetually broke ass lecture me about money. Ain't this some mess?

"Man, please," I say, pushing him aside to enter the steamy room. "You're the last person to give financial counseling to anyone. As much money as you borrow from me, I need to start charging your ass interest," I say, handing him his toiletry bag and towel while pointing him out the door. He can finish picking his Afro while he smokes a spliff in his brokedown van like he does every morning before he goes to work.

"You're right," he says, putting his foot in the door and preventing me from slamming it in his face. "So how about we make a deal? You can work for it by braiding my hair."

"Bryan, I've been trying to get you to pay me for hooking your bush up forever. Why the sudden change of heart?" It would be nice if he and a couple of his homies became my steady clients. Then I could really impress Netta with my skills and make some good money.

"Well, my new girl likes a neat man so I have to clean up my appearance a little. You know, just until I get the panties," he says, laughing at his own disgusting reasoning. I should've slammed the door on his foot while I had the chance.

"Bryan, you make me sick." Why are dudes so foul when it comes to sex? Are there any mature guys left in the world?

"So is that a yes or a no? I need the hook-up and I trust your hands. How about today after school? Don't act like you have something better to do," Bryan says, opening the door to his room and creeping in so he doesn't disturb Daddy and Jay sleeping.

"I'm not going to help you deceive some innocent girl into believing you're an upstanding young man when you're just as trifling as the dogs I have to deal with," I whisper before closing the bathroom door. I've wasted enough time talking to my uncle. His shady reasoning has put me in a bitter mood and I still have the rest of the day to go. I avoided drama yesterday by keeping to myself. But that isn't going to fly today and I need to be as calm as possible to deal with school.

"My girl doesn't need to know all of that. Why I do what I do is my business. And besides, this one's special. She might be your auntie one day. And if it works out, it's for your benefit. You'll have a regular customer for life," he says, coming back out of the room wearing a pair of wrinkled black Enyce sweats with a T-shirt to match. He throws his hoodie over his left shoulder before snatching his backpack from behind the bedroom door, heading outside.

"And what if y'all break up? You won't need my skills then and I'll be out of my regular pay." Having steady clientele is no joke. That's how a stylist eats and if I am going down that road, I've got to show him I mean business.

"Well, I'll still come to you when I want to look extra flyy," Bryan says, kissing me on the cheek while I set up my beauty tools on top of the closed toilet seat. At least when I'm at my mom's place, she has enough counter space for all my products. I barely have enough space for my lotion, deodorant, hair spray, and other toiletries, let alone extra room for the rest of my hair utensils. Depending on the day, I may need more to maintain my style than the cramped room allots.

"Fine, after school and it's twenty dollars. Cash only," I say. I actually feel relieved to have some income coming in this afternoon. This way I don't have to worry about buying my snacks throughout the day. I have AP meetings today and need the sugar to make it through.

"Cool, Jayd. And just to show how much love I've got for you, we'll name our first girl after you." He can be so silly sometimes. And knowing my luck, he'll probably have all boys, if they have any children at all.

"Never mind all that. Just get me my money and I'll be satisfied," I say, finally closing the door to get started with my morning routine. It's strange not having a boyfriend to dress up for anymore. I want to look good always, of course, but I don't have to worry about every single detail of my gear because no one's going to be that close to me at school. I wish I knew what was up with Rah and his silent treatment. I should've asked Bryan if he's heard from him, since that is one of his regular connections for herb, but he's already outside and I have to get ready before I'm late for school. I'll have to remember to have a talk with Nigel when I get to campus.

My first two periods went by okay except for the fact that Mrs. Malone hasn't finished grading my paper yet. I'm anxious to find out how I did on the rewrite. Maybe she'll have it for me at the AP meeting today at lunch, since the meeting at break was cancelled because Mrs. Bennett is absent today. I guess the AP English world comes to a halt without the chief bitch on staff to lead it. Her students must be happy to have a day without their shrew. I wonder if Mr. Adewale is sitting in for her classes.

"Jayd," Mickey says coming up behind me and practically pulling me away from my locker before I have a chance to lock it good. "Meeting in the ladies' room. Now." Whatever it is must be good if we're meeting in the bathroom. That's our spot to chat when we don't want anyone else to hear.

When we get inside, Nellie's primping in the mirror, even if her look is already flawless. The bathroom is fresh and cleaner than our bathroom at home. There's a couch in the small hallway leading to the sinks and stalls. All of the bathrooms on campus are nice, but this one is by far the best.

"I'm assuming you already checked the stalls," Mickey says, momentarily glancing under the ten adjoining doors before leaning up against the long vanity on the other side of the spacious room next to Nellie. When I went to a football game at Compton last year, I went inside their girl's bathroom and it wasn't nearly as clean or modern as this one.

"I know I'm fine enough to be a black Bond girl like Halle Berry, but don't get it twisted," Nellie says while brushing her long, jet black hair into a ponytail draped over her shoulder.

"Hell no, I didn't check the stalls and I've been in here an entire five minutes. No one's come in or out that I've seen."

"What's with all the secrecy?" I ask before entering one of the empty stalls. I might as well take advantage of the situation I'm in, even if I would rather be buying some CornNuts. Nellie, having the same idea, follows suit, leaving Mickey the floor.

"How late can I be before I should take a pregnancy test?" Mickey asks as I squat behind the closed door. I'm glad she can't see my face because if she could, I know I'd get a mouthful about my obvious disgust.

"Mickey, did I just hear you right?" Nellie steps into the stall next to mine and closes the door. "Jayd, do you have a tampon?" she says, reaching her hand under the wall and into my space. Reaching behind me to the small pocket on my backpack, I pull out a maxi pad and hand it to my girl.

"I only wear pads." Mama refuses to let me wear tampons because of the health risks associated with them. She says that's another thing that was wrong with my mama in high school. I sneak them in every now and then when I don't want to risk the embarrassment of spotting. But I don't like to wear tampons on a regular basis.

"Oh my God, Jayd. You really need to get with the times, girl," Nellie says, reluctantly taking it from me. But a girl can't be too picky in these types of situations. "This will last me until I can get to the nurse's office. I know she has a tampon in there."

"Uhm, hello. I just asked y'all a serious question," Mickey says from her station at the mirror. "How long should I wait before taking a pregnancy test?"

"Mickey, I thought you were smart enough to use protection. I know you've been with your man for a long time but I wouldn't trust him as far as I can throw him, and he's a big dude," Nellie says, beating me out of her stall. My Baby Phat gold belt is more intricate than it appears at first glance. Every time I wear this thing I feel like I'm trapped. But it seems like Mickey's the one caught up right about now. I'm with Nellie on this one. How could Mickey be so stupid?

"Look Nellie. Maybe that's how it works in your world. But we don't always know when we're going to do it, so my man may not have condoms on him at the exact moment. It's called spontaneity. Besides, a baby isn't the end of the world." Now I'm positive Mickey's not thinking straight. A baby right now would be the end of her world as she knows it. Not only would she miss out on our senior year of high school next year to change diapers, but if her man finds out she's been messing with Nigel at the same time, she'll really be dead.

"Are you sure he's the daddy?" I say, opening the cream-colored metal door and joining them at the sink to wash my hands. Her and Nellie stare at me in silence through the reflection in the large mirror. Nellie looks from me to Mickey, who's searching for the right answer in her head. But the look on her face tells me she doesn't know whose baby it is. "Damn it Mickey. You can't be serious."

"What, Jayd?" Mickey says, staring back at me through my reflection. Me and my girls make a pretty picture, but this isn't a Kodak moment. "You think I don't know how stupid I sound right now? I don't need either of you rubbing it in," she says turning off the faucet and shaking the excess water from her hands before walking over to the paper towel dispenser. "I just need some help."

Mickey's right. We shouldn't judge her, even if I did know something like this was going to happen. How could she sleep with both Nigel and her man without a condom, at the same time? And how could they sleep with her when I know they're all creeping too?

"Well," Nellie says, touching up her hair as the warning bell rings, announcing third period. Soon the bathroom will be filled with girls rushing to class. Our meetings usually take place before the madness begins. "They do have those test that can let you know as soon as three days after your missed period. How late are you?"

"Three weeks," Mickey says like it's no big deal. I know her mama got started early but damn, she needs to get it through her head that this ain't going to be no walk in the park. At least her mama knew who the daddy of her baby was.

"Three weeks? What are you waiting for Mickey, the baby to graduate from college? You need to go to the doctor as soon as possible," Nellie says. I'm glad she's here to handle damage control because I really don't want to be involved in this one, especially not after what Mickey's man said to me yesterday.

"Jayd, why are you so quiet?" I want to tell Mickey what happened but I don't know how to say it without incriminating myself in her eyes. The last thing I want to do is get into an argument with Mickey about her man but she needs to know exactly how foul he is for herself. "Can you please tell Nellie it's not that serious?"

"Mickey, it is that serious," I say, drying my hands and tossing the paper towels into the garbage before exiting the bathroom with my girls right behind me. "And you need to get all the tests they can run on you at the free clinic. You might be pregnant and no matter who the daddy is, the situation isn't good."

"What are you talking about? My man would take care of our baby. He takes care of me, doesn't he?" I hate to bring up her man's wandering eyes, but now is as good a time as any to call her out on her trifling man.

"Mickey, taking care of you is more than making sure your whip is clean," I say as Nellie grabs one more look in the mirror before following us out the door. The hall is beginning to fill with busybodies rushing to get to their lockers and I'm in no mood to be pushed around today.

"Yes, it's about taking responsibility and your man can't do that from his front porch," Nellie says, making a very good point. "How's he going to help you and your child if he can't keep his ass out of jail?" Unfortunately, like a lot of brothas I know, her man's addicted to the hustle of street life and jail is always in his future.

"Nellie, why do you always have to throw salt in my game?" Mickey says, stopping at her locker and turning the combination. "Besides, my man gets off house arrest in six months. After that he'll be able to get a real job and stop hustling." Mickey switches her books and checks her appearance in the small mirror hanging from her locker door.

"Six months? You act like that's around the corner," Nellie says, leaning up against the lockers and eyeing the crowd with me. I notice KJ and his crew walk in through the main entrance, still gleaming from their defeat over my boys the other day. I hope Jeremy's in a good mood in government class. Talking to him always makes the hour go by faster.

"The likelihood that he'll stop hustling just because you're knocked up isn't too good," I chime in. "He'll probably start hustling even harder if he knows he's got another baby on the way." I automatically glance down the hall to make sure my locker door is shut, which it is. Even nice schools have kleptomaniacs. Not that I have much to steal, but it would still creep me out if someone invaded my locker.

"Yeah, doesn't he have like two or three kids from his other baby mamas?" Nellie says, sending Mickey's already testy attitude into overdrive. If she is pregnant, it's going to be a long nine months.

"Look, I know y'all may not think he's a good man for me but he is," Mickey says, slamming shut her locker door and marching off toward her class. Nellie and I look at each other as if to say, "See what you did?" I know Mickey's pissed at us for telling her the truth, but that's what friends are for, even if she doesn't want to hear it.

"Mickey, wait," I say, grabbing her arm and stepping in front of her. I look into her hazel contacts and feel her pain and fear. I know she knows he's not good enough for her or her baby, no matter how much she tries to front. "I didn't want to tell you like this but your man made a move on me Monday when I tried to leave your house," I say, shocking Nellie. Mickey, however, looks anything but surprised.

"Your shit is way out of order, Jayd," she says, snatching her arm away from my hand and almost causing a scene. I knew I should've kept my mouth shut. "No matter what it seems like in your world, everyone doesn't want your ass." When the final bell rings above my head, signaling our tardiness, my friends walk off to their class and I go to mine without another word. What the hell did I just start?

As I turn back toward the main hall to get my tardy slip, because I know Mrs. Peterson will ask me for it, I notice the girl's bathroom door open and see Misty's head emerge before she races down the other end of the near-empty hallway. She looks at me and smiles deviously, like she knows our secret. Ah hell nah, she didn't hear us talking while we were in there. Mickey's business will be around the entire campus before lunch if Misty has anything to say about it, if not sooner. She and the rest of South Central have history class right now, my girls included. I hope Misty keeps her mouth shut for the time being.

"Jayd, what are you doing out of class?" Jeremy says as he walks into the hall from the office where I'm headed. "You're always on time. This must've been good," he says, holding one of the two doors open for me, allowing me to walk through. He's such a gentleman even when he's violating school rules.

"Too good," I say as we approach the attendance office. Usually a teacher wouldn't make me go through all this for being a minute or two late. But Mrs. Peterson would be all too happy to make me walk back to the office and bring an unexcused tardy slip back to class. I might as well save myself the walk and beat her to the punch. "And what about you? What's your excuse for being late?"

"Oh, I just got here. I almost didn't come but that would've meant missing the opportunity to sit next to you," he says, stretching his arms above his head while yawning. His faded Old Navy T-shirt lifts above his belt displaying his slightly hairy stomach and firm six-pack. I wonder if he realizes how strong of an effect he still has on a sistah. "What happened to us hanging out yesterday? Too embarrassed to chill with a loser?" he says, smiling his bright whites and sparkly blue eyes at me. Damn, the boy seems to get finer every day.

"No matter what you think of your skills player, you don't have game," I tease, taking the small pink slip from the student assistant and heading to class.

"Yeah, don't remind me," he says and I realize I've bruised his ego. He's still sore about losing the game against KJ a couple of days ago and I just rubbed salt in his wound. "I'll be the first to admit that KJ's got skills on the court, no matter how much of a jerk he is."

"Yeah, all too true," I say. Jeremy opens the door leading back into the main hall toward our classroom, across the courtyard. There's no one in the hall now except for us. If we could stay alone in our own little world we would probably still be together. "I've got to hand it to you. You've got some skills too, surfer boy," I say, gently bumping into him, making him lose his balance.

"Well thank you for the props, Lady J. But your boy needs

to be humbled." If Jeremy only knew the half of it. To let KJ's fans tell it, he hasn't lost a game of one-on-one in the past three years and he doesn't plan on breaking his record anytime soon.

"That'll never happen. Waiting for KJ to retire his ego is like waiting for OJ to admit he did it." Jeremy gently brushes his shoulder against mine, making me smile. I struggle to continue my thought as memories of our first kiss come into my mind. Why couldn't Jeremy and I stay in that moment forever? "If KJ's sure about one thing, it's that he's the greatest basketball player that ever walked the planet. If Michael Jordan walked in here right now, KJ would challenge him to a game and expect to win." Giving Jeremy a good laugh, we walk into the classroom and meet Mrs. Peterson's angry glare.

"Thank you for joining us, Mr. Weiner and Miss Jackson." Why does it sound so bad when she says our names together? I must've doodled them on my Spanish notebook a hundred times and they read well to me. "I trust you two know the way to the attendance office because I'm not letting either of you in here without a pass," she says without looking up from her usual post behind her desk. Her retirement cannot come soon enough. In fact, I'm going to throw her a going-away party, but she won't be invited.

"Here you go Mrs. P. No worries," Jeremy says, taking the pink pass from my hand and joining it with his before putting them both on her desk, wiping the annoying smirk from our teacher's face. Now if I had done something that audacious, I would've been in detention for the rest of the week.

"Don't make a habit of being late," she says, reluctantly looking at our passes before pointing us toward our seats. "You only get three tardies before a mandatory detention is issued. Now class, please write down your assignment and turn it in before the end of class. If you finish early, please work silently on your papers due in two weeks." Before Jeremy and

I can get comfortable in our seats, Mrs. Peterson looks up from her stack of papers and dead at me. "Miss Jackson, did you rethink your assignment?"

"If you mean did I choose to do my paper on a leader besides Queen Califia, the answer is no," I say, not backing down from her original challenge of my chosen topic. The class is silent and it's not because of the no-talking rule in her class once the bell rings—they're suspended in time, waiting for Mrs. Peterson to go off.

"Fine then. Have it your way. But like I said, this is a nonfiction report and you'll need to research and find supporting documentation. Fairy tales won't do." Jeremy and I look at each other and roll our eyes at her sarcasm. She's such a hater and everyone knows it. I don't know what's got her bra so twisted every day, but I hope she gets over it before she's the first person to croak from perpetual hating. She might be the first, but she probably won't be the last.

"Hey, don't let her get to you. You know you've got it going on," Jeremy says, making me blush. If Rah doesn't return my calls soon, he might lose some of his clout with me. Jeremy's a sweet guy and if I can give Rah another chance, I can certainly entertain the idea of giving Jeremy a second chance too.

I've been calling Rah for the past three days with no return answer or text. I know Nigel would have told me if it were something serious. So I can only guess Rah's silent treatment has something to do with his current ex-girl Trish. This brings back very unpleasant memories of the last time we were a couple. I don't know why he shuts down like this, but he's not getting away with keeping me in the wind for this long. I'm going to find out what's up with him one way or another.

During the long bus rides home, I had a chance to think

about my approach with Rah. I hate when he keeps me guessing. As I wash my hands in the kitchen sink, I see Bryan approaching the driveway. I hope he'll come clean with me if he knows anything about Rah's silence.

Making his way in from his day job at Miracle Market, Bryan throws his backpack down on the living room floor and takes a seat in front of the couch. I already put my stuff up in Mama's room, ready to braid his hair and grill him for info on Rah at the same time.

"Bryan, have you heard from Rah this week?" I ask, adjusting his head as I run the sharp comb down his scalp, making a clean part. "Damn. I forgot how much hair you have on your big-ass head. I should charge you for a head and a half." Thick hair runs in our family and braiding it is no joke.

"Less talking, more braiding," he says, picking up the remote control from the coffee table and leaning back into his chair. I grease his scalp and begin to pull the cornrows into place. This must be how a surgeon feels when she makes her first incision and then stitches it back to perfection.

"You didn't answer my question. Have you heard from Rah?" Mama already came in here once warning me not to get hair all over the living room floor. If she lets me work with Netta, she won't have to worry about it. Just like with Rah, I'm still waiting to hear back about that too. Mama hasn't said a word about it again and I don't want to call Netta without her permission. I'm learning patience but it's not easy.

"That's not your business and ease up on the pulling, girl," he says putting his hands on his head to relieve the pain. "Ouch Jayd, damn. Don't take your frustrations out on me." I push his head forward before untangling the crooked braid. He's right, I shouldn't take it out on him but I know he knows more than he's saying. I'm sick of this stupid code of

honor between dudes. Don't they know how much we sistahs worry?

"It is my business and I'm serious Bryan," I say, starting
the braid over, this time easing up on his scalp. "Have you
heard from him?"

"Yeah, okay. I ran into him yesterday on the courts by his
grandmother's house," Bryan says, relaxing back in his chair
again. "He asked about you. What's up with y'all?" He seems
to know more than I do. Why would Rah ask my uncle about
me but not return my calls? It's as if he doesn't want to have
contact with me and that's not the vibe he gave me this past
weekend. What's really going on?

"I wish I knew," I say, somewhat relieved that he's okay,
but even more confused as to why he's avoiding my calls.

"Jayd, I don't want to know the whole story, but I do know
the nigga loves you and wants what's best for you. Just trust
him and let him come to you when he's ready to talk." Bryan
may have a point. But I don't care how much he tries to defend him, Rah is wrong for making me worry. He knows this
is driving me crazy and he can only blame himself if he doesn't
like the way his little game plays out.

~ 4 ~
Foul Play

"You don't love me/
Yes I know now"

—DAWN PENN

After I finished braiding Bryan's hair yesterday, I helped Mama make dinner and then retired to our room to study, with still no word from Rah. I started to send Nigel a text, but I knew he would either be at practice or studying like I was and it wasn't that serious. He's well aware of his boy's disappearing acts and wouldn't entertain my panic for a second. I am going to make it a point to catch up with Nigel today. Rah can't ignore me forever.

This morning's unusually cool with no sun breaking through the gray clouds. I'm glad I packed my miniature umbrella and layered up today. Being caught in Compton without proper weather gear is one thing, but being by the beach where the air is cool and the sea breeze is already strong is a whole other experience. Jeremy sent me a text saying he was still good to pick me up in the mornings if I was okay with it. And truthfully, I wouldn't mind the chauffeur service at all.

"Watch the grass young lady," our crabby old neighbor Mr. Gatlin says from his driveway. He would be the only other person out this early in the morning to disturb my illusion of solitude. "Can't you tell by now when you're getting too close? These kids today ain't worth nothing." If he weren't my elder I would've cussed his ass out a long time ago. But

I'll leave that to Mama. She's the only one who can get him to shut up when he gets way out of line.

"Good morning to you too, sir," I say, making sure to step on the sidewalk directly between the two sides of his grass. This dude makes the craziest person appear sane.

"Never mind all that back talk, little missy. Just stay off of my lawn, you hear?" Shaking his rake in my direction as I continue to the bus stop, something catches Mr. Gatlin's eye, making him forget all about me.

"Good morning, Henry," I hear Esmeralda say from across the street. Her voice is deep and sultry and she doesn't sound like she's hissing, which is what I usually get. What the hell?

"Good, good, good morning, Esmeralda," Mr. Gatlin stutters. I don't know if he's afraid of her or nervous because he's digging her. But whatever it is, I know I don't want to know anything about it. My imagination is already running wild at the thought of those two together. Yuck. I can't resist asking Mama what she knows about this after school.

"Jayd, how did you get here before me and don't tell me your bus came early," Mickey says, blocking my locker. As cold as it is outside, she's wearing a jean miniskirt. At least she has on a North Face jacket with the chinchilla hood, but it doesn't make much sense to leave her legs out like that. Maybe she wants to enjoy the short and tight pieces of her wardrobe before her belly's too big to rock them if she's pregnant, even if that means turning into an icicle.

"I thought you weren't talking to me," I say, stopping in front of her as I wait to see if she'll move out of my way before I have to move her myself. Jeremy dropped me off in front because there was no parking and he needed to holla at Chance before school starts. I wanted to get to my locker and to class early for once this year, and now that looks like it's not going to happen.

"Whatever. Look Jayd," Mickey says, stepping to the side and letting me reach my combination. "I know you were right about my man hitting on you," she says, surprisingly calm. "This isn't the first time he's flirted with one of my friends and it won't be the last. I just thought he'd be more careful with you." I unlock the door and put my heavy backpack down on the floor. I don't have time to rationalize Mickey's behavior.

"Why would I be any different?" I ask, switching my books and notebooks for my first two periods out of the overstuffed locker and into my backpack. It's time to clean my locker in the worst way. With all the fliers and other crap that gets passed around this school, a girl's locker can fill up pretty quickly.

"Because y'all go to my school out of the hood. That's usually not his type, but I guess you're close enough to our hood for him," she says, popping her Big Red gum before continuing. "Also, I don't know if I should tell him about the baby just yet."

"Why not? Are you waiting for something to change?" I say, closing the metal door and heading out of the crowded hall toward the main quad. I wonder where Nellie is. Maybe Chance or her parents gave her a ride this morning. Mickey usually finds out the same morning if Nellie's going to need a ride from her. It must be nice to have so many options.

"I don't want to be just another baby mama to him. Maybe Nigel would be a different kind of daddy and husband," Mickey says, and I know where she's going with this. I can't let her take Nigel for a ride, especially if she's not sure he's the one.

"Oh hell no Mickey," I say, stopping in my tracks and looking up at her. "What would make you any better than Trecee if you played Nigel to be the daddy when you don't know if it's the truth?"

"Well, for starters, Nigel really could be my baby-daddy. It's no secret that my man's not the only one I'm dealing with," she says rubbing her flat stomach like she's nine months pregnant. This girl is crazy if she thinks it's going to be a big bowl of bliss being a teenage mother, no matter who the daddy turns out to be.

"Yes, and it's also no secret that your man's very dangerous. Do you think he's going to be happy that Nigel's the one you're claiming to want a family with? No Mickey, think about it. He'll kill Nigel over this and we don't even know if you're pregnant yet." I follow her out the double doors leading to the outside and push my way through the crowd of students rushing in. She stops at a tree to the side of the building and looks past me to make sure no one from our crew's coming.

"Yes we do," she says, taking a small piece of paper from her Gucci bag and handing it to me. "I went to the clinic yesterday. They said I'm about five weeks pregnant." Oh shit, now it's really on. Neither Nigel nor her man will take this news lightly. Even more importantly, how's she going to deal with the mess she's made?

"Okay, so what do you want to do?" I say, giving her back the positive test results and watching Nellie head our way. Nigel, Chance, and Jeremy aren't far behind, but stop to sweat Reid about something. I wish I could say that rehearsing with him is horrible, but it's not so bad. Reid's actually a good actor and since I already hate him, playing his wife isn't that difficult. It's Laura who's sending the hating vibes that make the days feel long. Every chance she gets she's showing off in front of Mrs. Sinclair and hanging on to Reid like I want her man.

"For right now, nothing. And please don't tell anyone, especially not Nellie. I don't want to hear her mouth about this yet," Mickey says, stuffing the paper into her pocket. There's barely enough room in that skirt for her behind, let alone anything else.

"Okay, but you know she's going to figure it out eventually and so will the boys." As Nellie approaches, I notice Misty, KJ, and the rest of his crew walk out of the cafeteria on the other side of the main quad. Misty looks our way but mainly at Mickey and gives her a devious grin. Before I can warn Mickey that Misty might know her little secret, Nellie walks up glowing, like she's the one with the bun in the oven.

"So, did you take the test?" Nellie whispers as soon as she reaches us. She acts like we're undercover spies on a mission. "Am I going to be an auntie?"

"It's too early in the morning for this conversation," Mickey says, avoiding the question and Nellie's eyes. Misty and KJ are staring at us in a way that lets me know they now both know about Mickey's baby. I've got to tell Mickey before it's too late.

"What are you waiting for, Mickey? These types of things don't simply disappear." Nellie sounds like her preachy self, which means we could have this same conversation for the rest of the day if Mickey doesn't tell her the truth, and soon.

"What's the rush in finding out? I'm still going to be pregnant whenever we find out." Mickey sounds naïve about this entire situation. It's almost as if some distorted version of her Cinderella story has come true. I know she thinks having a dude's baby will guarantee her financial security for life, but it won't. And hiding it won't help her either.

"Yes, but are you acting like it? You haven't even been to the doctor yet and that's not very responsible if you're going to keep it." Nellie steps up to Mickey and rubs her belly just like Mickey did a few moments ago. They're both acting crazy as far as I'm concerned.

"Of course I'm going to keep it," Mickey says, pushing

Nellie's hand away and staring her down. Jeremy, Chance, and Nigel walk up to us and notice the tension between Nellie and Mickey.

"Keep what?" Chance says, putting his arms around Nellie's slender waist. He bends down and rests his chin in the nape of her neck, making me miss Rah even more. Nigel pulls Mickey into him and kisses her hard on the lips, causing Jeremy and me to feel uncomfortable. The bell for first period rings and the students in the quad begin to dissipate. KJ and the rest of South Central linger behind and Misty continues her stare-down at Mickey. My Spanish class is across the walkway and I can run from here to there while the bell rings if need be and still make it on time, because I've got to talk to my girl.

"This new shirt I bought," Mickey says, looking down at her tight red shirt between kisses. "You like it? At first I thought it made me look fat but I think it's growing on me now." And that's not the only thing.

"Looks good to me," Nigel says, opening her jacket and eyeing her sparkly Apple Bottoms top. The V-neck cut is low, allowing Nigel a good view of her goods from his position, which he's enjoying. There's no shame in their game.

"Okay you two, that's enough. You're causing a scene," Nellie says, noticing Misty and company still staring at us from across the quad. I wonder how Chance deals with her tight ass sometimes. I guess he's glad to be dealing with any part of Nellie at all.

"I think they were staring before we came over," Nigel says. But Nellie's not amused. If I didn't know better, I'd think she was more jealous over Nigel than being overprotective of Mickey's virtue.

"Way to knock 'em up, man," KJ yells at Nigel, stopping the kissing marathon and looking past Mickey at his newly proclaimed enemy.

"Mickey, I need to holler at you for a minute," I say, trying to distract their attention before the secret's out. Maybe if she tells Nigel first it won't be so hard on him. But Nigel looks vexed enough to fly right about now.

"Yeah, go talk to your girls for a minute while I straighten KJ out," Nigel says, signaling his boys to follow him over to where KJ is sitting. Doesn't anyone have to go to class?

"Nigel, we're going to be late for first period. We can deal with him at lunch," I say, but he's not deterred from his goal. He looks back at me and smiles.

"Jayd, what's up with you? Are you really that worried about being tardy?" Chance and Jeremy look at me and then back to Nigel. "I'll walk you to class and tell Mr. Donald it's my fault you're late or you can just go. We got this," Nigel says as he walks across the grass with Chance and Jeremy by his side.

"Yeah, what's up with you, Jayd?" Nellie says and I know Mickey's going to be pissed at me, but it's better than Misty bursting her bubble.

"Mickey, I think Misty overheard us talking in the bathroom," I blurt out, trying to save precious time and my girl's secret at the same time.

"What? Are you sure?" Mickey says, charging after Nigel before I can answer her. I look back at Nellie, who's totally confused.

"So, what's the big deal?" Nellie says, still out of the loop. "It's not like Misty knows anything. We don't even know if Mickey's pregnant yet." I want to tell her so bad but it's not my place, it's Mickey's. Noticing my quiet response, Nellie runs after me as I take off after Mickey. "What is it, Jayd? What aren't you telling me?" I ignore her shouting, trying to reach Mickey before it's too late.

"Nigel, let's go," Mickey yells, but not before he reaches

South Central. The final bell rings above our heads, yet we all stay put. It must be nice being able to stroll into class any-time you want to because you're an athlete.

"Nah, not until we settle this once and for all." Nigel steps up to KJ, Del, and C Money, who rise to meet Nigel, Chance, and Jeremy's stance. They are all tall dudes, making me feel like a Lilliputian. Nellie and Mickey are taller than me but I know they feel small in comparison too.

"Want a rematch? You name the time and place and I'll be there," KJ says, his boys laughing behind him as they walk off to class, leaving my boys behind.

"Westingle, next Sunday afternoon. Don't be late," Nigel yells after them. Chance and Jeremy look at each other and then back at Nigel. They have no idea what they're getting themselves into. Playing ball in Redondo Beach is one thing. But playing ball on the Black side of town is going to blow them away.

"Your loss, man. I wouldn't miss it for the world." KJ may be cocky, but Rah and Nigel have been playing on their home turf forever and have total confidence when they're there. I'm sure Jeremy's going to get the boot as the third person now that it's a game on familiar ground, which is unfortu-nate because between the two white boys, Jeremy's got the most game, on and off the court.

"Hey Mickey, when's the baby due?" Misty says, giving Shae and Tony a good chuckle. Without any warning, Mickey lunges at Misty, causing Misty to run away—or get into a physical fight with Mickey, and I know she doesn't want that.

"Come back here and say that shit to my face," Mickey says as Nigel holds her back from running after her prey. "Tricks are for kids, Misty. When are you going to grow the hell up?"

"Temper, temper," KJ shouts as the rest of his crew slowly disperse to class. I hope my boys kick his ass.

"I gotta roll," Jeremy says, hitting Chance in the shoulder

while indicating he should get to class too. They have English
with Mrs. Bennett first period and even if she is cool with
them, she's never completely chill about the school's rules.
After all, she is the chair of the AP department and has to set
an example of perfect bitchiness for the rest of the teachers.

"Yeah, we'd better get going. You want me to walk you to
class?" Chance says to Nellie, who's still shocked at Mickey's
reaction toward Misty. I guess since Mickey might be pregnant, in her view she should also act like it. Wait until Nellie
finds out Mickey really is pregnant; then the judgment will
go into overtime. I can already tell Nellie's going to be the
auntie from hell in Mickey's eyes.

"Yes, thank you, baby. See y'all at break," she says, turning
her attention toward Mickey and me. I look at Mickey, who
has managed to wrestle free from Nigel's grip, but not for
long.

"Mickey, can I talk to you for a minute?" Nigel says, obviously not letting Misty's comment go. He can feel something's up by the way Mickey went after Misty.

"I have to get to class. I'll see y'all at break," I say, escaping
before I get dragged into this mess any further. "I'll tell
Mr. Donald you've got my back for this one." It's bad enough
Mickey told me she's not only with child but that her plan is
to con my homeboy into turning the maybe-baby into his;
she swore me to secrecy on top of that. What the hell?

Since we had such bad luck with a nosy-ass Misty over-
hearing us in the restroom, we opted for our next favorite
quiet hangout by the library. I finally got my English paper
back. Mrs. Malone wasn't as vicious with her red pen this time
around, but I still only got a B-minus—my lowest grade in
her class to date. I just can't get into what I'm not feeling,
and sometimes that means taking the lower grade.

"I told Nigel about the baby," Mickey blurts out before I

can open my pack of peanut M & Ms. I'm craving nachos but the student store was out of them so I opted for chocolate instead. Today I'm craving my favorite foods, like I'm the one expecting.

"Why would you do that when you don't even know if there is a baby yet?" Nellie says between sips of her sparkling water. "Or if he's the daddy." I look at Mickey sitting next to Nellie and Nellie looks at me for validation that she's right. I look at Mickey and hope she tells our girl the truth before I crack under the pressure.

"There is a baby and Nigel is the father," Mickey says biting the head off her Drumstick ice cream cone like it's the best dessert she's ever tasted. From where I'm standing, Mickey already looks like she's eating for two. I don't know how long I'll allow Mickey to live in her fantasy world where she was a virgin until she met Nigel, but I'll play along for now. At least she told Nellie half the truth.

"Yesterday you weren't sure who the father was. What changed?" Nellie asks, rising from the small bench they're sharing to join me at my post up against the shade tree. I've been sitting all morning and need to stretch my legs. Even without Nigel as my escort, Mr. Donald didn't trip on me for being late because he was too busy grilling another student about her attitude. I still need to holla at Nigel before the day is over. I'm getting some information out of him about Rah if it's the last thing I do.

"What changed is my priorities," Mickey says, giving us both an evil glare. She already knows how I feel about it and she knew that Nellie would definitely have a problem with her trickery too. "You were right. My man's not going to be the best father and as the mother I get to decide what's best for my baby and that's Nigel as the daddy." We stop talking, allowing a few students coming out of the library to pass by.

When they're out of earshot, I say, "Like it's really that simple." My girl's living in la-la land if she thinks everything's up to her. "Fathers do have rights, you know," I say, though by the look in Mickey's eyes, I know she's not hearing me.

"Jayd, ain't nobody worried about the father's rights. The daddy is who I say it is and neither one of them can prove any different." Devouring her cone, Mickey sits unaffected by her fictional world. I know she can't believe that either her man or Nigel's going to give her any child support without knowing if the baby is theirs beyond a shadow of a doubt. They both must have more sense than that.

"So you've never heard of a paternity test?" I remind her, snapping Mickey out of her personal reality and back into ours. "You know they require those before they grant child support."

"Yes, but there will be no need for all of that," Mickey says, opening her bottle of Mountain Dew and downing three big gulps. "Nigel's so sprung on me he's ready to break up with Trish for good and make us permanent. We're going to be a family."

"Mickey, do you honestly think I'm going to stand by and watch your foul-ass instant family pop up while you punk one of my best friends?" Who does she think she is, the knocked up version of Cinderella?

"He's your friend, but he's my man," Mickey says, giving me a sly smile I've never seen before while taking out the silver MAC case from her purse. "Who do you think he'll believe?" Mickey says, licking her lips in the compact mirror. Now I see she's really tripping. "Me or you?"

"You can't do this to him," Nellie says. She's so upset she's spitting water as she talks. "If you don't tell Nigel, I will," she adds, stepping up to Mickey like she's ready to go to blows with her. Damn, all I need is my girls at each other's throats again. We barely made it through our last fight unscathed, I don't know if we can survive another one so soon.

"Whatever, Nellie," Mickey says, rolling her eyes at our girl while she puts her makeup back in her purse and takes a sip of her drink. "Like he'll believe a word your little sell-out ass has to say." Nellie takes another step forward and Mickey looks at Nellie, daring her to take the first blow.

"Mickey, you're not thinking clearly," I say, stepping in between them to diffuse the situation before it gets too ugly. "You were all over Trecee for lying about KJ being the father of her baby. Why would you turn around and pull the same shit?"

"Because this is completely different and I'm not lying. There was no chance that KJ could have been the father of her spawn," Mickey says, rising from her seat and dusting the crumbled peanuts from her ice cream off her miniskirt. "As far as I'm concerned, Nigel is the daddy," Mickey says, rubbing her flat belly. I can't imagine that nine months from now Mickey's going to be somebody's mama, especially not my homeboy's baby. "Don't ask me how I know but I can feel it and I'm not going to be a fool and let him slip away from me." Nellie backs away from Mickey, realizing now that our girl has completely lost it. "And why aren't y'all getting on Nigel? His behavior was just as foul as mine."

"Yes, but he's not being deceitful to cover it up," Nellie says. Having had enough of Mickey's ghetto logic, Nellie begins to walk away from the library toward the main quad where we can see everyone hanging out and enjoying the cool, sunny day, including our boys. By the time she makes it all the way over to where they're standing, break will be over. Watching Nellie approach them, the boys look up and notice our hiding spot. Mickey nods at Nigel who begins to head our way. Good, he'll save me the walk. I want to get my inquisition about Rah out of the way early.

"I'll see you after school Jayd," Nellie says over her shoulder, nearly jogging to where Chance is waiting with Jeremy. I hope she doesn't open her mouth, at least not yet. Truthfully I would prefer it if Nellie did let it slip rather than me having to tell them. The best thing is for Mickey to be honest about the entire situation, but I'm not going to hold my breath waiting for that to happen.

"Don't hate the player Nellie. Hate the game," Mickey shouts after her as she gulps down the remainder of her soda. Nellie looks over her shoulder to throw Mickey one last evil glare before meeting up with her man and my ex.

"Why are you being so nasty with her? She's just trying to help you," I say, tossing my trash into the wastebasket by the front door. I wish I could toss her ass in there for the way she's acting but I can't. She was there for me when I needed her and she even came through for Nellie after the madness that girl put us through. Now it's our turn to help her see straight.

"When has Nellie ever tried to help anyone of her own good will?" Mickey waits a second for me to answer but I've got nothing. "Never, and this time is no exception," Mickey says, picking up her book bag from the ground next to her feet and putting her arms through the straps. "She wants another chance at Nigel and this is her perfect opportunity to make herself look good and me like a slut."

"Mickey you don't really think that, do you?" I say, amazed at how quickly she is ready to misjudge her best friend. Her and Nellie are tight and keep each other in check. But right now Mickey's the one who's out of line. "Nellie has done more for you than she has against you. You shouldn't be so quick to turn on her."

"Have you forgotten about what we just went through with that girl? She turned on us at the first opportunity to hang out with the rich girls. That's who she is—a wannabe—and I'm not letting her at my man." Damn, this is getting too serious too soon. And speaking of moving too fast, here comes the reason we're in this mess to begin with. I told Nigel and Mickey I didn't like the idea of them dating, but nobody ever listens to me until it's too late.

"By the way, your other man, also known as your maybe baby-daddy, is on his way over here." Chance and Jeremy both nod a "what's up" at me as I watch Nigel approach.

"It's not a maybe anymore, Jayd. I really am pregnant," she says, sounding more like she's trying to convince herself than me.

"I know that, we've got the proof. But the father's identity is still up for grabs, no matter what you say." Mickey glares at me hard as Nigel moves in. His face is more sullen than usual. I know he must be tripping over Mickey's revelation and worried about his girlfriend's reaction to the news too. I'd hate to be in either of their shoes right now.

"Well, tell him I'll be right back. I've got to pee," she says, racing through the library door to use the restroom. It's going to be interesting to watch her growing belly develop. I hope her moral compass grows a little too.

"Hey, Jayd. What's going on over here?" he says, giving me a hug and looking over my shoulder. "And where did Mickey run off to?" Nigel looks toward the library, knowing she wasn't in a rush to check out any books. That's not our girl's style.

"Oh, just girl talk. Mickey had to use the bathroom. What's up with you and your boys this morning?" It's ironic that he, Chance, and Jeremy have become homies, but not surprising. They are the most popular dudes up here, each with their own unique flow, which makes them equally desirable. Chance is the silly but cute white hip-hop rich kid, but not as wealthy as his half-Jewish surfer counterpart, Jeremy. And well, Nigel's the black quarterback hustler from the hood, making him the most wanted of the trio. They make an irresistible crew. No wonder KJ and his boys feel so threatened by them.

"Well, I guess you know about the baby," he says, instantly looking like an embarrassed little boy who got caught with his hand in the cookie jar, this time literally. What is it about getting girls knocked up that brings out the innocence in these dudes?

"Yeah, I do. You and KJ have something else in common besides being good athletes," I say, not wanting to rat my girl out but making sure Nigel doesn't get played in the process. I've known him longer and my loyalty is slightly torn between the two of them. Like Nellie said, if Mickey doesn't come clean to Nigel, I will tell him myself, but not yet. I'll give her the chance to be honest about the situation before it completely blows up in her face.

"Oh yeah? What's that?" he says. I forget he came in a few weeks after school had already started, missing the first week of drama I went through with KJ and his crazy almost baby mama, Trecee.

"Girls all over the world would line up at the chance to have your baby. It must make you feel good to be so wanted. Just be careful not to get caught up while you're out here creeping," I say, shifting my weight from one foot to the other, as if the slightest difference would give me some sort of height advantage to look him in the eye. Like most people I meet, Nigel's much taller than I am and looking up at him for too long makes my neck hurt.

"What's that supposed to mean?" he says, folding his arms across his chest and cocking his head to the side with a very serious frown on his face. Despite his irritation, he looks cute in his orange FUBU sweat suit. I love how his chocolate brown skin looks in bright colors and the way he dresses. I also like the same things about Rah.

"Just what I said. You know I've got your back no matter what," I say. Now he looks hella confused. "But that's not what I want to talk about," I say, quickly changing the subject before Mickey returns. "What's up with your boy and don't act like you don't know who I'm talking about." I know he doesn't want to let go of what I just said to him but he knows better than to avoid my questioning, especially if it's about Rah. Looking defeated by my stare, Nigel relaxes his stance and begins to share.

"All I know is that Sandy and Trish got into it at Westingle on Monday. It was pretty bad," he says, shaking his head from side to side.

"Sandy," I say, surprised to hear her name. She was my Misty before I got to South Bay High. When she first came to Family Christian, I befriended her crazy ass only to find out she slept with Rah—who was my boyfriend at the time—in the boy's locker room and had his baby nine months later. After she gave birth to their daughter, she tried to use the baby to manipulate Rah but it didn't work. She ended up moving suddenly to keep Rah from his daughter. Just the thought of her makes my blood boil but it doesn't change the way I feel about Rah right now. "When did she get back in town and what does that have to do with him not calling me all week?"

"I'm not sure when Sandy got in town and neither is Rah. He was just as surprised as we all were to find out she was back," Nigel says, glancing toward the library door, anxiously awaiting Mickey's return. He seems nervous about seeing her and he should be. Like Sandy, Mickey can be vicious when someone gets in the way of what she wants. But at least she's not crazy. "All I know is that Trish got messed up pretty bad and had to go the hospital. Why he's not calling you I don't know anything about." So Rah is getting my messages and he's all right. I admit I'm relieved to know it's not about us, but in a way it is and until I get the full story from him, he's on my shit list.

"Please let Rah know that he's in hot water with me and

the sooner he calls, the better it'll be for him." I look at Mickey push through the door and she doesn't look so good. Her hair looks a little tangled like she just stepped through a whirlwind or something. Maybe she got sick and had to throw up again. Comes with the territory for her. I guess being pregnant isn't as cute as she thought it was going to be.

"Yes sir, Jayd sir," he says, saluting me like I'm his general before Mickey tucks herself under his arm, staking her claim. I hope that possessive display isn't for me because she's got another thing coming if she thinks a broad can come between Nigel and me. We've already been down that road before and I'm the one still standing. I need to get out of here before I'm late for government class. Jeremy's already left his post by Nellie and Chance, who are making the most of their time together. I hope she doesn't risk Chance's heart to get a shot at Nigel, as Mickey thinks. I don't want any of my friends to get hurt in the mess.

"At ease, private," I say, slapping his hand away from his forehead. "Just make sure Rah gets the message." I choose to ignore Mickey's attitude and walk to class. It's funny how dudes act when they want to be with you, but have a strange way of keeping their distance when things start to get too serious. Until I hear from Rah, I'm pushing him way down on my priority list. I have to get through the rest of this school day. I'll worry about our relationship after the final bell of the day rings.

~ 5 ~

From The Sidelines

*"I was your baby, baby, baby, baby/
When you needed hugging."*

—ANGIE STONE

For the rest of the school day I felt like I was in a time warp. Sandy being back in Rah's life isn't good for anyone, especially me. There's nothing I can do to help Rah if he doesn't tell me what's going on first. Plus I need to talk to him about Mickey's baby. And I can't help Nigel without ratting my girl out. It feels like my hands are tied and my friends are the ones holding the rope.

As I walk down our block I can't help but remember Esmeralda and Mr. Gatlin's strange exchange this morning. I wonder what kind of noose she's got around his neck. They say that there's someone for everyone but I don't think that's true. If it were, me and half of the people I know wouldn't be in the messes we find ourselves in on a regular basis. Getting closer to Mama's house, I notice two Compton police cars parked on the street and in the driveway. This can't be good. They never stop by to say "what's up" in our hood. The neighbors are all outside watching the drama unfold. I hope Mama didn't go off on another one of Daddy's women.

"Jayd, your grandmother said for you to go straight to the backhouse when you get home," my neighbor Brandy says from her seat on the porch. I was half expecting to see my Uncle Jay sitting next to her, smacking on the barbeque ribs and coleslaw she's having for dinner. I'm assuming we'll be eating takeout at our house tonight too.

"Thanks, Brandy." As I get a little closer to home I see Rah's red Acura parked across the street. I guess he got my message from Nigel. Rah's used to the constant arguing at my house so whatever's going on won't be new to him. It's still embarrassing that my family has to have the cops come and solve our family battles sometimes, but at least we're not alone. Almost every household on this block has the same issue.

Walking up the driveway I can see inside the dining room window where the officers are taking a report from my Uncle Junior. It looks like this battle was between my uncles this time and not my grandparents. Mama and Daddy are probably the ones who called the police. Ever since my uncles started to use weapons on each other, my grandfather has stayed out of their fights, and Mama was never in them to begin with. If she could, she'd make a potion to vanquish them all from her house, Daddy included. But it's not in her heart to do that—at least not yet.

"What's going on in here?" I say as I open the garage door to see Bryan, Jay, and Rah sitting in a circle eating Subway, one of my favorite meals. If Rah thinks he can butter me up with food, he's only partially right. It's going to take a whole lot more to get back on my good side than a value meal. It is a good start though, because a sistah is hungry. I didn't want to spend the money I made braiding Bryan's hair on food and the lunch we have during rehearsal isn't all that. The booster club moms who provide lunch are into the healthiest, nastiest food available and I can only take so much of it.

"Eating, that's what. And staying out of the line of fire," Jay says, smacking on his chips while talking to me. "Let's see what else is on," he says, reaching over the small card table to the black-and-white television propped up against the wall.

"How was school?" Bryan asks, trying to bridge the gap between Rah and me. He knows we haven't spoken all week and I'm hot about it. If Bryan and Jay weren't here, I would have ripped into him from the door. But per Mama's suggestion, I'm trying to keep a cooler head these days.

"School was school," I say, sitting down in the empty seat across from Rah, who's in a daze and waiting for me to make the first move, his usual mode of operation when he knows he's wrong. "What's going on in the house?"

"Your other dumb-ass uncles got into it over the iron," Bryan says, totally unaffected by his older brothers' behavior. We're all used to their shit.

"There's blood all over the carpet," Jay says, leaning back into his seat before picking up the deck of cards in front of him and dealing them counterclockwise. Daddy taught us how to play Spades, Bidwiz, and Blackjack when we were younger. Now we're both pretty good at the card games.

"It's only a few drops. You exaggerate the truth worse than a chick sometimes," Bryan says, taking his cards and putting them in order. By the way he's organizing his hand, we must be playing Spades. I pick up an unopened bottle of water from the table and begin to drink while making myself comfortable. If Rah doesn't pass me my food soon I'm going to snatch it away from him without saying a word.

"And what are you doing here?" I say to Rah, who hasn't stopped looking at me since I sat down. He hasn't picked up his hand yet either. From the way we're seated, we're forced to be partners. I hope he came with his A game because he knows I play to win.

"I came to talk to you but I think your grandmother needs your help in the back. Here's some dinner for you. I thought you might be hungry," he says passing me the six-inch veggie and cheese sandwich with cheddar cheese and sour cream Ruffles in the bag. This is my favorite Subway meal and I love that he knows that. I can tell by the look in his eyes he's mournful, but that won't be enough to appease my hurt.

"Thank you, I guess," I say, not easing up a bit. I'm so mad at him I could spit. But before my rudeness can get the best of me, I hear Mama walking from the backhouse into the garage. She's probably been waiting for me to get home so I can help her in the spirit room. I didn't even get to change out of my school clothes before being summoned to work. And who knows how long the police will be here.

"Jayd, you can talk to them later," Mama says, entering the dimly lit room. I can tell by her voice she's in no mood to bargain with me but it's still worth a shot.

"Mama can I eat first? I'm really hungry and I just sat down." Bryan, Jay, and Rah look at me like I just signed my own death certificate. Before I can apologize, Mama walks across the garage floor to look me in the face. I know I'm in for it now.

"We have work to do," she says sternly, eyeing each of us before walking out the back door toward the spirit room. I guess me grilling Rah will have to wait until later if I want to live long enough to do it.

"Damn Jayd, you've got some big balls for someone so little," Bryan says, making us all laugh. They wouldn't dare question Mama and usually neither would I. I really want to eat and vibe with Rah but Mama's work always comes first.

"That's what makes her a queen," Rah says, passing me my bottled water. "I want to talk to you about this week," he says, rising to walk me out. Even when we're seated I feel like a midget next to him.

"So talk," I say, getting up from my seat before putting the food into my backpack and walking out the back door. Bryan and Jay look at Rah as if to say "I'd hate to be you right now" and they're on point with their feelings. There's no way I'm letting Rah slide on this one. "I've been calling you all week. Did you get my messages or is your phone broken?"

"Jayd, come on. I hate it when you're mad at me," he says, taking my hand and spinning me around to face him. He smells so sweet and fresh. I want to hug him and fall into his arms, but I can't. Not yet. "Listen to me."

"Listen to you say what, Rah?" I snatch my hand away from him and cross my arms around my chest. I have to get to the spirit room; I've kept Mama waiting long enough but I need to wrap this conversation up real quick.

"Jayd, just give me a chance to explain." Rah puts his hand on my shoulder and I almost give in—almost.

"Why should I when you can't keep your word to me? It's okay for you to shut me out of your life when it's convenient and then come waltzing back into mine when you're ready?" I pause to let him respond but he's too shell-shocked to say anything so I'll have to answer for him. "Hell no, Rah, it's not okay with me and my feelings aren't a faucet I can turn on and off at your command."

Mama comes back out of the spirit room to empty a bucket of water into the adjacent garden and to call for me again. Noticing Rah and me in a heated conversation, she gives me a look letting me know I need to wrap it up, and soon.

"Jayd, I know I messed up. But you know how Sandy is and with Trish getting hurt fighting her I guess I just didn't want you to be next." His eyes say sorry but his logic is still way off.

"Next? Don't you mean first?" I say, reminding him that I've already been through hell and back with him over Sandy's crazy ass. "You're treating me like I'm sitting on the sidelines watching the show, but I'm not. I'm right in the middle of your tired-ass game and I'm sick of playing with you."

"Jayd, wait," Rah says, pulling me back, but I'm done talking for now. "It's not like that. You know you mean everything to me. Can we just talk about this, please?"

"Everything? If I mean so much then why did I have to find out what's going on in your life from Nigel?" Silencing him for the time being, I walk toward the backhouse ready to clear my head and help Mama clear hers. Rah knows better than to come back here without my or Mama's permission. Unless invited by one of the Williams women, the spirit room is no-man's-land and they all know it.

When I finally reach the backhouse, Lexi's in her usual spot resting across the threshold, effortlessly ushering me into Mama's therapeutic fortress. The entire space isn't much bigger than our living room but is packed with a lot more stuff. All of Mama's spirit tools are neatly organized, which makes it cozy and warm in here. The same scent of night-blooming jasmine and honeysuckle that's ever present in Netta's shop lingers in this small room as well. The warm air and sweet smells instantly calm my nerves, causing me to momentarily forget about Rah and my hungry stomach. All I want to do is be in here and help Mama work. As soon as Mama looks at me, I remember questioning her in front of the boys and feel instantly ashamed.

"You can eat first if you need to," Mama says from her station at the sink. She runs the cold water across her hands and stares at me for a few moments before looking away. She's sorry too and I feel her pain. Her sons have hurt her yet again and her one female ally in a house full of men would rather hang with the boys instead of doing the women's work required to heal the household.

"No thank you. I'm good," I say, closing the screen door behind me. I can hear the garage door shut and then the back gate. Rah has left for the evening, leaving me to my work with Mama. She's already lit the candles, giving a golden hue to the already yellow walls. My normal spot at the table is already taken by Mama's many tools. This is my safety zone from the crazy world outside.

Before I can get in the room good, my phone vibrates.

When I flip it open, Rah's name appears on the screen. Now what?

"Peace, Jayd. We're not done talking. See you tomorrow after school. I love you, girl."

Why do I keep letting him back in after he hurts me? Maybe it's because I know it's not intentional, but that's still no excuse. Rah should know better by now than to leave me hanging. And if he really loves me then he should respect my feelings, not just do what he thinks is right. I fold up the phone and slip it into my purse, ready to give Mama my undivided attention.

"Why do we deal with men?" I ask Mama as she dries her hands on a yellow kitchen towel before passing me fresh white clothes to put on. I'm not sure exactly what we're working on today, but from the looks of the ingredients spread across the kitchen table, it must be heavy.

"The better question is why do we allow them to deal with us?" Mama says as she chops up several bunches of fresh spinach from the garden. She also has a bowl of boiled eggs, cinnamon sticks, a grater and other dishes, scallops, fresh shrimp and fish on ice, five jars of honey, and a large machete with a big bottle of palm oil next to it.

"I feel you, Mama," I say, putting my backpack and purse on the shelf closest to the door.

"You see how your uncles act and yet they each have women running after them like they're God's gift to the universe." Mama's on point with that one. Each of my uncles except for Bryan and Junior have baby mamas that would fight over them in a minute, and I don't why. I'll be damned if I'm going to fight over a dude who's still living with his mama in his thirties or even twenties, for real. "Those trifling-ass fools were in my house fighting over whose turn it was to use the iron. Now mind you, it's my iron but like a bunch of toddlers, they decided to claim it and throw a tantrum when someone else wanted to use it."

"Mama, easy on the spinach," I say, hanging my shirt and jeans over the top of the white bamboo Chinese screen before opening it and joining Mama at the kitchen table. She's diced the spinach up so finely, it's almost liquid. "Did anyone get hurt?"

"Yes," Mama says, passing me the cinnamon sticks and the grater. Why do I always have to do the menial task? "As usual, your Uncle Junior got his ass kicked." Being the smallest of the lot, Junior always loses against any of my other uncles but he never presses charges. I don't even know why they bother calling the police.

"He looked okay when I saw him talking to the police," I say, grating the cinnamon into a glass bowl. It smells so good and refreshing. I swear, doing the work is half the healing process for me.

"You should have seen him a few hours ago. I think he may have broken a tooth and he doesn't have any insurance or money to get it fixed. At first I thought he broke his nose but the paramedics said it's okay."

"The paramedics?" Maybe Jay was right about the blood on the carpet. It wouldn't be the first time. We really should have hardwood floors, especially in the den, where they all sleep. It's so disgusting back there I never go in there unless Mama sends me to get something, like the iron. I'm glad everyone has cell phones now because it used to be a regular trip to go back there to get the phone. Now I don't know what it looks or smells like in the den and it's much better for me if it stays that way.

"Yes, child. Your Daddy had to call 911 to get those boys to stop fighting and by the time he did, Junior was already bleeding all over the place. Even if I'm not the one they hit, I feel like I'm the one being beaten and I'm tired of it." Mama places the spinach into an oversize wooden bowl and begins to peel the eggs from their shells. I feel sorry for whoever's on her bad side right now because Mama's hotter than usual.

"I'm sorry, Mama." I never know what to say in these situations to make her feel better. I wish I could take her out of our house and move her into a space of her own. She deserves to be at peace and free from the negativity surrounding this house.

"Jayd, it's not your fault. And running from the problem won't do any good." How did she know what I was thinking? Mama looks up at me and winks, forcing both of us to smile. "You forget I brought you into this world in more ways than one. I may not be able to read your thoughts like your mother can, but I can still read you, little girl."

"Yes, ma'am," I say, grating the last of the cinnamon while Mama places the eggs around a brilliant brass and white porcelain serving plate before generously coating them with honey. She then takes the spinach, shrimp, scallops, and fish and places them in the center of the dish and sprinkles everything with the fresh cinnamon and more honey. This dish must be for our spiritual mother, Oshune.

"So what else is going in your world besides you and Rah fighting?" she says, cleaning up the mess we've made and directing me to do the same. I'm not sure where to begin. There's so much going on between my friends and as always I feel caught in the middle.

"Well, Mickey's pregnant," I say, only slightly shocking Mama. She knows Mickey and Nigel have been seeing each other for a while and that Mickey has a boyfriend. "To top it off, she doesn't know who the daddy is and has decided by default that it will be Nigel." Mama looks at me and then down at her loyal German shepherd Lexi who's up and ready to follow us out of the door.

"Jayd, I've heard enough. You and your friends are always

in some mess. I thought y'all were smarter than that and I know you are because I raised you better than that," she says, putting her hands on her hips and pointing her long finger-nail at me like I'm the one bringing home the baby.

"Why are you mad at me? I didn't do anything," I say, toss-ing the last of the eggshells into the trash can. Mama cleans the table with a wet rag and Pine Sol while I get the broom and sweep the floor. The strong smell of the seafood and egg platter only slightly permeates the thick, fragrant air. It's about nine o'clock, which means I only have another two hours to get my homework done and my outfit picked out for tomorrow if I want to get to bed on time.

"Exactly my point. You didn't do anything at all to help your friends but went out of your way to help your enemy," she says, referring to Misty as she rinses the worn dishrag in the sink. I look at Lexi, who's eyeing me as if to say, "Don't look at me. You know she's telling the truth." A sistah can't get any love around here.

"Mama, that was different. Misty and her mother were about to be put out of their home. I was just trying to help." I should've known better than to make a gris-gris for Misty and after the way she called me out at school, I've learned my lesson.

"Well, maybe if you had put more energy into helping two of your best friends it would have worked out for everyone." Mama can be a cold sistah when she wants to. "Learn your lesson this time around, Jayd. We don't want to have to go here again."

"She's right, Jayd. You can't save the world, but you can help the people closest to you," my mom intervenes. I still can't believe I'm getting lectured for my friend's pregnancy. What the hell?

"Oh Jayd, there's always something going on in your world, my little fire child," Mama says, placing the heavy dish in the center of the table and eyeing her magnificent creation.

It is a pretty offering. "Ask for protection from other people's problems when we present the sacrifice to the shrine. You're going to need it now more than ever before." She then takes the machete and palm oil sitting behind the door and leads me out of the spirit room. "It's time to go back inside. I'm sure everything's calmed down and the cops are gone." Mama doesn't deal with cops any more than she has to. "Please cover the plate with a paper towel and bring in Oshune's offering."

As we walk across the backyard toward the main house, I notice Esmeralda's profile in the window across the yard. Just the thought of her being in close proximity to us gives me chills.

"Did you know there are people who are jealous of babies born with cauls? They get hated on for no reason, as you would put it," Mama says, carefully holding the huge knife as she walks past the garage, headed for the backdoor. "They would do anything for the blessing you and others like you were born with." Others like me? She's never put it quite like that before. I know there are stories of other gifted people born with the veil at birth but I've never met another one that I knew of. We should have a support group or something for all the drama we have to put up with on a regular basis.

"How do I protect myself from the haters? Can you make me a permanent charm or gris-gris or something?" I ask, making Mama laugh. Her mood always improves when she gives offerings to the shrine.

"All protection starts by feeding your Orisha and asking Legba to cool the road for your success. That's why we're feeding Ogun and Oshune tonight. We want their blessings and protection in this crazy house and from our crazy neighbor. You can start working on your own charm after we're done." Damn, I asked for more work so I really can't say anything about this one. But something must've gone down that I don't know about to make her give me an assignment like that.

"Did something else happen?" Mama looks at me and the

plate of food in my hands. It looks like she doesn't want to tell me but has no choice now that I've asked. Mama's excellent at evading the truth when necessary, but she's a horrible liar.

"Misty's mother was over there today and I saw Misty go in a little while before you came in. They're up to something and I'm pretty sure it has to do with you."

"What are we going to do?" I know Misty isn't happy about me interfering with her problems and that she will retaliate but I don't know how. Whatever she's up to must be serious to have Mama worried about it.

"We'll act when the time is right. But for now we will just watch and see. Keep your eyes and ears wide open, Jayd." Mama climbs the three steps up the back porch, finally reaching the door. Before entering the kitchen, she peeks in through the window to make sure the coast is clear. Everything appears to be quiet inside for the time being.

"But the longer I wait the more time she'll have to implement her revenge," I say, following Mama into the house. As we walk through the living room I notice the red speckles across the faded blue carpet. I look up and focus on the back of Mama's head where her cornrows are intact, taking my mind off the bloodshed in here just a few hours ago. Mama opens her bedroom door and the candlelight guides us to the altar, where we are ready to let go of our problems.

"Sometimes the ones on the outside looking in have a greater advantage than those right in the middle of the madness." Mama's right. I have to look at the entire view and not just do what I want to, especially in this situation with Misty and Esmeralda. Whatever Misty's planning must be good if she hasn't let it slip at school. For the next few days I'll take Mama's advice and get to work on protecting myself from the guaranteed ricochet of Misty's actions. I don't want to accidentally get hit by her fire.

~ 6 ~
The Rebound

"You kept on thinking that you were the only one/
You were too busy thinking that love is a gun."

—SADE

After Mama and I finished our ritual last night, I did my homework and went straight to bed. I ran late this morning because I didn't pick out my clothes before I went to bed last night like I usually do. When my morning doesn't start out right, my whole day's messed up and today is no exception to the rule.

Rah and I didn't have a chance to finish our talk about Sandy and Trish or more importantly, about us. He texted me late last night saying he would pick me up from school today and give me a ride to my mom's house, like nothing's happened at all this week, but I can't let this one slide. If we're going to have an honest friendship, he's going to have to treat me with the same respect he does Nigel. Otherwise we're wasting our time pretending to rebuild something we never had to begin with.

"Jayd, what's up with you? You've been off all day," Jeremy whispers in the dark rehearsal room, grabbing my hand and pulling me into his arms like we're still together. Oh no, he didn't go there with me. I'm glad one of my friends is interested enough in my acting to come to some of the rehearsals, but claiming me is not part of the production. He feels so good I let him hold me a moment too long before I put him in check.

"What are you doing?" I say, pushing away from him. His eyes look surprised at my reaction but his smile says he was half expecting it. No matter how distasteful it may be in his opinion, he likes to see me hot.

"You looked like you could use a hug. I was trying to be a good friend." Jeremy looks slightly wounded but he'll have to get over it. I'm tired of being there for dudes when they're ready to be intimate, but won't share important aspects of their lives with me. Coming from opposite sides of the track, Rah and Jeremy have a lot in common.

"A good friend keeps his hands to himself at all times," I say, trying to keep my voice down as Reid and Chance perform their scene. I know Chance is acting but I'm sure the vehemence in his voice is real.

"You don't mind it when Chance and Nigel hug you, or even Rah," he says, getting to his point. He wants to know how close Rah and I are and I'm not telling him a thing. I can't talk to Jeremy about my relationship with Rah or any other dude. We're not that friendly.

"Jayd, you're up next," Matt whispers from the side seats where he and Mrs. Sinclair are seated. Seth is backstage controlling the lighting and sound. Between the three of them, our in-house plays are always well done. Reid and Chance are the best enemies I've seen on stage in a long time. It's as if all of the pent up animosity they have toward each other comes out in the scenes they're in together. Overall I think we're going to have good reviews for our performances.

"Jeremy, you and I agreed to be friends and that's what we're doing. So, no more close embraces or questions about my other friends. And for your information, I'm doing fine. I just have a lot on my mind," I say, leaving him posted up on the back wall while I tiptoe backstage to wait for my cue.

These boys are too confusing. It's enough that I have to deal with Rah in a couple of hours, but Jeremy's flirtatious behavior is enough to drive me over the edge.

"Fine then, don't tell me. But I'm only a phone call away if you need to talk," he says heading toward the side door, ready to beat the bell for fifth period. It was nice of him to keep me company but I don't want anyone getting any more mixed signals from me. If I'm going to figure out this thing with Rah, I've got to stay focused and keep my emotions from bouncing around like a basketball.

And speaking of rebounds, Rah and I have to get it straight once and for all what his true intentions are with me. He's not the only one in this relationship and he needs to start acting like it right now.

My dance workout today was much more vigorous than usual and it was just what I needed. We're doing a section on South American dances and I'm loving the Brazilian music our teacher brought in for us to rehearse to. It really got my blood flowing and now I feel like I can take anything that's coming my way, including a battle with Rah. I took my time walking to the main hall from sixth period in the hopes I would get some quiet time before Rah picks me up, but not today.

"Jayd, we hardly saw you at all today. What's up?" Nellie says as she and Chance meet me at my locker. Nigel and Mickey are at the other end of the hall getting her stuff out of her locker before we all head out of Redondo Beach for the weekend. I don't like being near the water when it's cold like today. It'll be a good ten degrees warmer by the time we reach Inglewood. My mom has another weekend full of activities planned with her man so it's just me and my spirit and schoolwork since I have no job to go to. As long as that last paycheck from Simply Wholesome is at my mom's house when I get there, it's all good. They can act funny-style and force me to quit all they want to as long as they don't mess with my money.

"Nothing much. You know how Fridays are for me: quizzes and turning in assignments," I say, reminding them both of how easy they've got it. "What did I miss?"

"Oh, just the usual bitchy bickering," Chance says, eyeing the crowded hall as students get ready for the weekend. The marching band passes through, ready for the football game tonight. I switch out my books for the weekend and shut my locker door. It's a disgrace. I have papers from the first day of school crammed into the overstuffed space, making it look messier than need be. Usually I'm pretty good about keeping it clean but I've been so distracted by all the other priorities in my life that I've forgotten to keep my own messes straight.

"Yeah, Mickey and Misty went off on each other at break. You should've been there," Nellie says, all too excited. She and Mickey aren't speaking right now and Nellie is back on her hating path. Mickey and Nigel eye us from down the hall. I assume they're deciding on whether or not to join us. Even if I do agree with her, I still think Nellie shouldn't hate on our homegirl. We just have to figure out a way to get her to tell the truth to Nigel without destroying our friendships.

"Yeah, and who were you rooting for?" I say as I turn around to walk toward the office. As I approach the other end of the hall, Rah walks through the double doors, looking good in his silver Phat Farm sweat suit and baseball cap to match. How can I stay mad at him when he always looks so flyy?

"Myself, as always," Nellie answers, walking behind me hand in hand with Chance. Rah stops to greet Nigel and Mickey, who are still at her locker as we walk up, creating more tension where there should be peace.

"What's up, y'all?" Nigel says, unaware of the battle going on between us girls. I wonder if he knows Nellie's still feeling him. Probably not, and if he does he couldn't care less. Mickey's got him sprung and vice versa. All would be cool with that if they weren't involved with other people.

"Hey Nellie, Chance, Jayd," Rah says, looking at me intently as Jeremy walks up behind him, making this scene even more awkward. "You ready to roll?" Before I can answer Chance greets his boy, causing Rah to look over his shoulder at my ex. They stand about the same height and I look up at them both, not sure what to say. I know Jeremy wants to talk but Rah is now my steady ride to Inglewood on the weekends and I don't want to mess that up.

"What's going on?" Jeremy says, giving the eye to Nigel and Chance and nodding "what's up" to Rah. He and Rah are cordial, but ever since Jeremy and I broke up, Rah hasn't had anything nice to say to or about him. "Are we ready to kick KJ's ass on the court next weekend?"

"Fo' sho', man. He's not winning shit on my home court," Nigel says as cocky as ever. I hate to be the bearer of bad news, but KJ's skills are not confined to a particular space. He's hot no matter where he balls and he knows it. If he wins at Westingle a week from Sunday, Nigel, Jeremy, and Chance will never be able to live it down.

"What are y'all talking about?" Rah says, out of the loop. Sometimes I forget he doesn't attend South Bay, as often as he's up here.

"Man, that punk-ass nigga got us in a game of three-on-three with his boys Monday, but it's cool. We got next," Nigel says, wrapping his arm protectively around Mickey's waist while rubbing her belly. How long is she going to play this game with him? "We're going to clean the court with his face when he comes to our side of town."

"Yeah, that's right. We can take him," Chance says, trying to make Nigel's move on Nellie but she's not having it. She abruptly moves his arms from around her waist to her shoulders. Nellie's too prude to display a lot of public affection with Chance. Something tells me if it were Nigel she might feel differently.

"The hell you can," Rah says, laughing at their team spirit. "If you want to win against black men you have to play with black men," he says, pretending to shoot a basketball in the air while walking toward me. Rah puts his arms around my waist and kisses my neck, taking me and everyone else by surprise. It feels good but he's way out of line and I don't want Jeremy to think we're together when we're not.

"Why are you all over me?" I say, pushing away from Rah and smacking him in the arm. He gives me a wicked smile and gets back to the conversation. I notice Jeremy's tight jaw loosen slightly and he breathes a deep sigh of relief witnessing my reaction.

"Damn man, it's like that," Chance says, feigning hurt. He knows how it is when it comes to sports and black dudes' ego. They feel superior and most of the time rightfully so. But this time Rah's in for a surprise.

"Hell yeah, it's like that. I don't have to see it to believe that KJ and his boys whipped your asses. I've seen them play. They were probably being nice." Rah can be a real jerk sometimes and—unfortunately for me—it's part of his appeal. "You know white boys can't jump. Ain't that right, Nigel?" Nigel looks at Chance and back at Rah, who's waiting for his brotha to back him up, but not this time.

"Man, normally, I'd agree with you. But Chance and Jeremy can ball, real talk," Nigel says. Mickey smacks her chewing gum loudly, annoying Nellie, who doesn't need any more aggravation from her. Nellie stares at Mickey and then at Nigel. I feel like she's going to spill the beans any moment. But before she has another opportunity to blow Mickey's façade, Mrs. Bennett walks into the hallway from the side entrance,

ruining our impromptu school session. Now it's really time
for us to go.

"Oh look, students who love school so much they're here
fifteen minutes after the bell has rung on a Friday afternoon.
What are the odds?" she says, breezing by us in the now near-
empty hall on her way to the office. Rah laughs at her comment and everyone but Jeremy and I follow suit. Mrs. Bennett's
not in their lives like she is in ours.

"We're just chilling, Mrs. B," Jeremy says, taking some of
the heat off me. Stopping in her tracks, Mrs. Bennett spins
around like a ballerina, looks over her thin-framed glasses,
and smiles at him.

"Jeremy, I've known you and your brothers for years and
I'm always surprised by the company the three of you choose
to keep." The insult rolls off her tongue like water and lands
on my head, setting me off.

"Why do you bother being nice to this woman?" I ask Jeremy,
and he looks at me as if to say "shut up." This is why we broke
up in the first place. He'll never be cool with me speaking my
mind when he doesn't agree with what I have to say or how I
choose to deliver it.

"This woman," Mrs. Bennett says, placing one of her hands
on her thin hips, tilting her short frame heavily to her right
side. Her blue eyes shimmer in the fading sunlight, appear-
ing as a blue-green color, almost mirroring Esmeralda's eyes.
"I deserve more respect than that, young lady."

"Whatever," I mumble under my breath. I don't want to
start another war with Mrs. Bennett but she makes it so easy
to hate her. My friends look in silence, waiting for the next
move.

"Jayd, why do you possess so much animosity toward me?"
she asks, taking a step closer to me. "Maybe you need to spend
more time getting to know me before you're so quick to

judge me as your enemy." Something in Mrs. Bennett's cold eyes is more familiar to me than usual. I feel like she knows more than she's saying but I don't know what about. "Have a nice weekend, everyone, and do be careful," she says, turning around and walking off toward her original destination.

"She's a piece of work, isn't she? I'm glad she's not my teacher," Nigel says, hugging Mickey tightly before they walk off. "See y'all later."

"Yeah, we'd better be out too. There's a sale at Nordstroms and I don't want to miss it," Nellie says, pulling Chance in the opposite direction. I wonder if Chance knows he's being used. I'm sure Nellie likes him, but not as much as she's apparently still feeling Nigel.

"Later," I say. Now it's just me, Jeremy, and Rah, who's waiting for Jeremy to walk away but he doesn't. He stands across from us looking at me like he has something to say but can't find the words. I hope he stays on mute because now is not the time to make a scene.

"I hope you didn't take my comment about white boys ballin' too seriously, man. It's nothing personal," Rah says, crossing his arms over his chest. I switch my backpack from one arm to the other, ready to go.

"Not at all. And I hope you don't take it personally when we prove your theory wrong," Jeremy says, also crossing his arms over his chest. This conversation is about way more than basketball. After Rah found out Jeremy was embarrassed by what he considers to be me and most other sistahs' strength, he's no longer cool with entertaining Jeremy. I'm sure he wouldn't be welcome at a session anytime soon.

"Yeah okay," Rah says, laughing at Jeremy's statement. "Are you ready, queen?" Rah says looking down at me. I see Jeremy's jaw tighten again and I know this isn't the end of the battle. I also have a feeling Jeremy was going to offer me a ride home before he realized Rah is now my designated escort.

"Yeah," I say, following Rah toward where his car is usually parked. Jeremy doesn't move and his eyes make me want to hear him out. "Can you give me a minute please?" Rah looks back at me and Jeremy, not wanting to go, but he respects my wishes and leaves me to talk to my other ex. What can he really say? He spent the majority of the week dodging me because his baby mama jumped his soon-to-be ex-girlfriend. Me talking to Jeremy is the least of our problems.

"I'll start the car," he says, eyeing Jeremy hard before leaving us to talk. I don't know exactly what Jeremy has to say, but I want to hear it.

"You can do better than him, you know," Jeremy says, smiling in that cocky way that drives me mad. Where does he get off judging my friends?

"Jeremy, you can't honestly stand here and tell me I can do better than Rah. You don't even know him." He'd hung out at a couple of sessions at Rah's house but that's not enough to warrant a comment like that. He's just hating on Rah and that's not cool.

"No, but I know you and I know a girl on the rebound when I see one." What the hell did he just say to me? I wouldn't be on the rebound if he'd behaved better when we were together.

"I was on the rebound when I got with you, so what's the difference? It seems like we're always on the rebound."

"No, that's not true. Only when you care about someone does the rebound take effect and I know you cared about me and still do." Jeremy takes a step closer to me, breathing heavy. If he moves any closer my face will be in his chest, making it very easy for him to kiss me.

"Jeremy, you and I both know we're too different to be together and that's that."

"So you choose to go backwards because he's familiar? That's not the Jayd I know and love." Did he just say that he loves me? I'm standing in the empty hall looking for the cameras to catch this practical joke on film but there are none. This shit is real and it's making me dizzy.

"Stop saying you love me," I say. Once was enough and I didn't take him very seriously then. "You don't even know what love is."

"I don't? How would you know if you don't give me another chance to prove it to you?" Being in love sounds nice, but in my experience it's way overrated. And people seem to fall in and out of love like it's a roller-coaster ride at Six Flags. And I'm not down for the ride anymore.

"You'll only love me if I conform to your versions of right and wrong and I can't do that," I say, walking past him and heading for a waiting Rah. "I wish it were different Jeremy, but I'll always be me and I like myself just the way that I am."

"I know that," he says following me. "I admit it's a lot to deal with but I'll learn." I look back into his eyes and see that he's sincere in his gesture, no matter how unknowingly demeaning it is.

"I don't want you to have to learn and I damn sure don't want to see that look on your face like you had when I spoke back to Mrs. Bennett." The look on his face now confirms my feelings. "Let's just be friends but without the judgment. See you Monday," I say.

Jeremy's mouth is wide open as I leave the empty hall, ready to deal with Rah too. They both need to know where I stand. Neither one of them are ready to devote themselves fully to a relationship but don't want anyone else to have me. On the rebound or not, I don't want to be anyone else's rebound either. And we're going to get to the bottom of Rah's issues once and for all.

~ 7 ~
Hoodrats Wear Prada

"I'll take your man."

—SALT-N-PEPA

"So what was that all about?" Rah says, putting the car into gear as soon as my behind hits the seat. Jeremy followed me out to his car parked across the street without saying another word. Rah's vexed and he has no reason to be. But boys will be boys, I guess.

"Damn, can a sistah get in the car all the way before you pull off?" I barely had a chance to close the door shut and he's already at the stop sign.

"You know I don't like to be kept waiting," he says, blaring the radio as loud as he can. He's not drowning me out this time. I reach for the stereo knob and turn the volume down, causing more heat from an already pissed Rah. "Jayd, I know you know better than that, girl," he says, returning T.I. to his loud volume, again trying to drown me out. He's the one who should know better. If I've got my mind set to something, there is no music loud enough to silence me.

"You can be as mad as you want but we're talking about this now," I say, pushing the sound off completely. Rah speeds ahead toward the beach and I wish I could jump in the water like the surfers in the distance. Jeremy's probably on his way there now to free his mind in the waves. I admire the freedom his lifestyle allows him. But no such luck here. Rah and

I have a different reality and we need to get in sync or we'll have nothing left to look at together.

"What's up with you and the white boy?" he says, getting right to the heart of the matter. One thing I can count on from Rah when he does decide to share is brutal honesty always.

"We're just friends," I say, telling the truth though Rah doesn't look like he's buying it. He abruptly makes a right turn onto Pacific Coast Highway, causing other drivers to honk their horns at us. Even the bike riders and rollerbladers look crazily at the red Acura Legend flying down the busy street. The windows have limo tint so they can't see who's inside but I'm sure because of the appearance of the car and the loud bass rattling the trunk they know two things: the driver is young and male. Guessing he's black is also a bet they're probably willing to take.

"Okay black man, act out if you want to. But you know these Redondo Beach cops would love to give your ass a ticket, so keep playing," I say, crossing my arms over my chest and looking out my window. Unwillingly heeding my advice, Rah eases up on the gas pedal and relaxes his grip on the leather steering wheel.

"Don't tell me you're just friends, Jayd, when we both know that's B.S.," he says. His phone vibrates on the dash, making me jump. "Are you back to kicking it with that punk after he already showed you his true color?" He turns down the phone and throws it back on the dash. He must be really hot to toss the Samsung like that.

"No, Rah, and there's more to Jeremy than his shortsighted view of my attitude." I can't believe I'm defending Jeremy to Rah when I know Rah's right. I shouldn't even entertain a friendship with Jeremy but I can't help it. Just like I can't explain my attraction and patience for Rah, I can't explain it with Jeremy either. "He's my friend and he's a good person.

You've hung out with him before and you know I'm telling the truth."

"No Jayd, I don't know that. All I know is how he made you feel a couple of weeks ago. Maybe you're the one who needs reminding of who your real friends are and who's simply frontin'." After a few moments of silence Rah's phone vibrates again and this time he answers the call.

"What's up, man?" Rah says. "I'm headed back to Jayd's mom's house now and then to the pad. Are we still on for tonight's session?" He must be talking to Nigel, which reminds me I need to holla at Rah about Mickey's master plan.

"Tell Nigel I said hi." I reach into my purse and pull out a half-eaten pack of Starburst. I usually eat the pink ones first because they're my favorite. Back in the day I would take out all the red ones and save them for Rah. But now I eat the whole pack myself without a second thought.

"Alright man. I'll holla at you tomorrow. You take care of your baby and Jayd says what's up. Later," Rah says, hanging up the phone and returning it to the dashboard. "Nigel said 'what's up' and he'll see us at the session tomorrow. He and Mickey are staying in tonight." If only Nigel knew it might not be his baby he's taking care of—that's where Rah has to come in whether he wants to or not.

"Did you ask Nigel how he knows the baby's his when Mickey has another man she's dealing with?" Rah stops at the red light and turns to look me in the eyes. I don't know what he's searching for but his look tells me he can't believe I just asked him that question. I don't know why he's so surprised when he knows how the games are played out here.

"I don't have to ask my nigga nothing like that. Is there a reason I should?" The light turns green and I wonder how far I should go with this conversation. I don't want to insult Nigel's intelligence nor Rah's fragile ego when it comes to his boy, but somebody has to say something before Nellie does. If she spills the baby beans it'll sound like hating and this is too serious for stupid beef.

"Well, it doesn't seem smart to claim a baby that might belong to another dude, especially a notorious gangster like Mickey's man." I cross my right leg over my left and straighten out my Guess jeans and sweatshirt. It was too chilly to wear my sandals today so I opted for my Nikes, even if they do need cleaning. Mama would kill me if I walked outside with my feet uncovered in this cold air. If I caught a cold I'd never hear the end of it.

"I can't call it, Jayd," Rah says. He looks like he's thought the same thing himself though, and I know I'm on the right track. Maybe he'll convince Nigel to hold off on happy family plans until a paternity test can be done. "My nigga's not dumb."

"I know that, Rah, but he's not thinking clearly about the entire situation." Rah looks torn between what he knows is rational and being a good friend. "I know you don't want to call him out, but what if the baby's not his and he gets caught up paying child support or even worse, marrying Mickey?"

"Wait a minute," Rah says, waving his hand like I've committed a serious foul. "This is your homegirl you're talking about. Why would it be so bad if they did raise the baby and get married? That's a happy ending, ain't it?"

"Hell no," I yell so loud the people riding in the car next to us turn around and stare through the top of my cracked window. Rah promptly rolls it up from his driver's side controls and turns the air on low. "There are no happy endings when friends of mine are being deceived. I've known Nigel for much longer and what Mickey's trying to pull is wrong." Damn, I let too much slip and suddenly, rather than having an innocent conversation out of concern, I've turned it into an act of disclosure.

"What are you talking about, Jayd?" he says turning onto Aviation Boulevard, where we can see the airplanes lined up for takeoff from LAX. I wish I could get on one of those jets right about now. "What's Mickey trying to pull?"

"Nothing, Rah," I say, trying to clean up my slip. I'm not going to let Mickey get away with this for too much longer but I also don't want to be the one to rat her out. It's a thin line between helping and hating. "I'm just saying that Nigel should get a paternity test for everyone's sake."

"You know what it is." T.I. announces a call and I dig into my purse searching for my cell. I hope my man gets off on those gun charges. Not that I think T.I. should be out buying guns or nothing like that. But my brothas are always getting caught up in one way or another and just like Mike Vick, the haters will blow it out of proportion and try to make him pay well beyond what he deserves.

"Damn, Jayd, you need to clean out your purse," Rah says as I continue to search for my phone. Before I can get to it, it stops ringing, and luckily too. The call was from Jeremy. I wonder what he wants to talk about now. He saw me leave with Rah and knows how long it takes to get to Inglewood from school, so why would he call knowing I'm still with him?

"I know that smart-ass," I say, silencing my phone and continuing our talk. "But for real, talk to your boy about it. He has his whole life ahead of him and many more baby mamas in his future, I'm sure," I say, trying to make Rah laugh and not think too hard about Mickey's plotting.

"He doesn't want any more baby mamas, just this one." He looks at me from the corner of his eye and turns onto Century Boulevard, almost at my mom's. "Did I ever tell you that Nigel got this girl pregnant last year?" Now that's news I never heard.

"No, you didn't but we weren't exactly talking then, re-member?" He and Nigel ended up leaving Family Christian at the same time I left and came to South Bay High. We didn't rekindle our friendships until Nigel ended up leaving Westingle to come to our school last month, so I'm out of the loop on a lot of things I'm sure.

"Right," he says, remembering our bitter break-up over two years ago. "Well, the chick decided to have an abortion even after Nigel swore to take care of her and the baby. I think he sees this as a second chance for him." That explains his attitude toward Mickey and her growing belly. "No matter what girls may think, niggas have feelings too, especially when it comes to our seeds." I know he and Nigel are good brothas and good father material too.

Rah pulls up in front of my mom's house and turns off the engine. We both meditate on what he just said. Nigel has it really bad for Mickey, I know, but this situation isn't good and it can only get worse the way it's going.

"What does Tasha think of the new baby?" I ask as we exit the car. Rah grabs my weekend bag from the backseat and I take my backpack and purse from between my feet and step onto the curb.

"She doesn't know and doesn't care. Nigel broke up with her already." Damn, I guess he is serious about making Mickey his only wifey and I bet she thinks she's hit the jackpot, at least until her man finds out. I'm sure she hasn't been as forthcoming with her man as Nigel was with his girl.

"I'm tired of this subject and of talking, period," I say crossing the quiet street toward my mother's apartment building. I want to take a shower, do my hair, and go to bed. I did promise Rah I'd braid his hair for a set amount of twenty dollars before I settle in for the evening. If I can get five or so steady clients, I can easily make up for my pay at Simply Wholesome, and then some. If Netta lets me work with her, I can make even more money, bringing me that much closer to my transportation freedom.

"You still gone braid my hair though, right," he says, leaning into me to give me a kiss as I unlock the multiple bolts to my mother's home, but I'm not in the mood.

"Yes, I am a professional. But don't think I've forgotten about your disappearing act this week or your rude behavior with Jeremy. You need to get over yourself for real, Rah, if we're going to stay friends." We enter the small apartment and feel the warmth of the sweet-smelling space welcome us in.

"Well, I guess I'll be getting over myself then. Won't I, queen?" Making himself comfortable on the floor while I get settled and get my hair bag from the hall closet, I realize friendships are too valuable to be wasted but are constantly tested. And, like all challenges, I will rise to the occasion, even if that means getting hurt in the process.

After braiding Rah's hair, we ordered a pizza and kicked it for a little while. I can do my hair tomorrow since I don't have to work. I might go up to the restaurant and holla at Sarah and Alonzo one of these days—I miss working with them. Rah being here made me forget about how upset I was when I first opened my check, but now it's time to kick him out. No matter how cool my mom is he can't be here if and when she decides to come home from her date. We got everything straight but the issue between Nigel and Mickey, which we agree to disagree on.

"Look Jayd, I wish I could explain it but I can't. When Sandy told me she was pregnant I knew the baby was mine. I don't know how, but I just knew and she wasn't innocent either. If he wants to be her baby's daddy, then let him. It's none of our business." I remember having this same discussion with him when he found out he was going to be a daddy. Again Rah tried to keep it from me but Sandy wasn't having it. She fronted me at lunch in front of the entire school where I was the only one out of the loop. We got down to the root of our problems that day and I didn't speak to him again until he found me through Nigel. And here we are having the same conversation about our friends.

"It is our business. That's what friends are for," I say, playfully pushing him in the arm with my shoulder. Rah responds by holding me down on the couch and tickling me.

"Rah, stop! Let me go," I yell at him. He eases up and lets me off the couch. "You know it's time for you to go now, right?" Half of me wants him to stay but the other half knows we need to call it quits for the evening.

"Yeah, it's about that time I guess," he says glancing at his watch. "Are you going to walk me down? You know the rats come out at night." Rah gets up from the couch and stretches his arms over his head, forcing his Ecko T-shirt to rise slightly above his jeans. The thin hairline on his chiseled stomach has always been one of his most attractive features to me.

"What rats? The neighborhood is rough, not dirty." Rah smiles at me and reaches over my head to grab his jacket off the hook next to mine.

"Not those rats, silly. Hoodrats," he says, making me laugh. "They can be more dangerous than the real things." Rah's right about that. It ain't nothing like having a broad who's pretty, fights like a dude, and doesn't give a damn about no one but herself on your bad side. Everyone has their own definition of a hoodrat, but none of them are good. "So are you going to walk me down or what?"

"Yes if you agree to talk to Nigel," I say, rising off the couch and passing him up to grab my sweater before opening the front door. It's getting hot in here and I know it's not the heater's fault. The November chill in the air reminds me that I need to invest in a heavier coat but I don't have any extra cash, even if I did just get paid. This is the wrong time of year to be out of a job.

When we walk outside, Rah leans in for a kiss again and this time I let him. I have missed his soft lips. He picks me up in his muscular arms and kisses me like we're the only two people in the world. Coming up for air, we look at each other and smile. When I think we're finally in heaven, a girl's voice screams from behind us and I'm back in our woman-made hell.

"After all that I've been through for your ass you're still getting your hair braided by this wench," Trish says, pointing her crutch in my direction. How did she find out where my mom lives? She quickly limps up the driveway with Tasha right by her side. They're both dressed in black from head to toe, with their Prada handbags to match. I don't understand how girls who have this much money can be so petty. You can take the girl out of the hood but you can't take the hood out of the girl, no matter how expensive her wardrobe is.

"Trish, what the hell are you doing here?" Rah says, protectively stepping between us in an attempt to block me from his girl's anger. I wonder if he did the same thing for her when Sandy was attacking her. Knowing Rah, I'm sure he did his best to keep them both from getting hurt and feels bad he couldn't do more. "Shouldn't you be home resting?"

"The real question is how she knew where I lived." I step around Rah and face Trish eye to eye. I understand how she feels having to deal with Sandy and all. But coming up in my space where she's not invited is a bit much for me. This snooty broad needs to know she too has limits, especially where I'm concerned.

"Don't worry about all that," Trish says. I know she doesn't want to mess with me but she's about to get another ass whipping if she doesn't tone her attitude down. "I told you I don't want you seeing her anymore and that includes getting your hair braided. I told you my little sister can braid way better than she can," Trish says, looking at me in disgust. I know she's not hating on my skills.

"You need to get out of my driveway now before your other leg gets hurt," I say stepping toward her. Rah tries to block me from attacking her but I'm way too vexed to be held back. Tasha steps in front of Trish to protect her but she's no match for me either. It's almost one in the morning and these tricks are on a stakeout over a man. What the hell?

"Trish, have you completely lost your mind?" Rah says. "This isn't the time for this conversation and you're way out of line. I can get my hair braided by whoever I want and I told you I'm going to see Jayd, no matter what you say."

"But I took a beating for your ass. And it looks like y'all are doing much more than braiding." Trish is too pretty and prissy to be in this mess but like other hoodrats, she can't help herself. I know Sandy's crazy ass had to have overwhelmed her. Sandy's energy is so powerful, she must be the closest thing to a tornado in human form.

"And I've kicked Sandy's ass over him before, so what's your point?" The mention of Sandy's name alone makes my head even hotter. If Trish says another word to me, it's going to be on. Completely ignoring my comment, Trish continues to question Rah.

"I thought you said one of your homeboy's girls was going to braid you up tonight? How come I was on my way to pick up Tasha from getting her hair braided and I see your car parked around the corner? I know you don't have any friends on this side of town." Girls in Trish's zip code only venture to Inglewood to get their hair braided or visit dudes they probably shouldn't be seeing. She looks me up and down like I smell bad. The yellow streetlights provide only a small amount of light but I hope it's enough for her to see the disdain in my eyes. Did Rah really lie about who's braiding his hair? That's not cool with me at all.

"Trish, go home. You're making a fool of yourself," Rah says, taking a step toward her. Tasha steps in front of her friend, blocking Rah's move. Rah looks down at her, knowing if he wanted to move her five-foot-two frame he could, with little effort. He looks over her head at a stone-cold Trish. I don't know what he ever saw in this girl. Her hair has blond streaks that always need a touch-up, she looks tired and hungry, and she sounds like a dude. But I do have to admit she's got that Jada Pinkett body going on, which excuses all of her other flaws in a dude's eyes, I guess.

"Not until you leave first. And Rah, my brother, will be hearing about this." If her brother weren't—in a way—Rah's employer, she wouldn't have any power over him. I'll have to get to work on helping him while I study my own potion-making this weekend.

"What the hell do you think I was just doing? Go home. We'll talk about this later," he says, looking from me to her. I've had enough of this scene and I'm tired. She's lucky I don't have to get up for work in the morning. Otherwise her ass would have been really cussed out. As her and her girl hobble back down the driveway, I turn around to walk back upstairs without saying good-night to Rah. How could he lie about me to her? I thought he was supposed to be so up-front and honest with her about us? Come to find out it's all just another game to him.

"Jayd, wait," Rah says following after me. But what can he say? Trish's got him through her brother and I don't know what I want to do with him. Part of me feels like he brings this madness on his own head and I don't know if I can make a potion to help him with that.

"Why, so you can lie some more?" I can see the downstairs neighbor's light turn on. I knew we would wake someone up with our noise. I hate being the cause of any drama, especially at my mom's house. She likes to keep her business out of the mouths of her neighbors when possible.

"What are you talking about? I never lied to you," he says. I turn around halfway up the stairs and put my hands on my hips, shooting him a piercing look.

"Did you lie about me braiding your hair?" Rah looks at

me and shakes his head from side to side. He looks down at his feet and holds the rails with both his hands, leaning back and taking a deep breath. He looks up at me with a stare I can't read. Does it bother him that he lied to Trish or that he hurt my feelings?

"I just told her that so she wouldn't sweat me. What's the big deal?" he says, shrugging his shoulders. I walk down the two steps between us and get up in his face. I want him to hear me loud and clear without me having to yell. Why do I feel like I'm training him on how to be a good friend? Shouldn't he know this by now?

"The big deal is that I deserve all the credit for my work." I can't explain it but it's more than the credit that pisses me off. There's something very intimate and powerful about braiding and I don't appreciate him not being proud of me as the weaver of his crown.

"Hey Jayd, did I hear right?" Cedric, my mom's downstairs neighbor, says out his front window. "You braid hair? How much for fifteen cornrows straight back?" Rah looks at me sternly and I know he's already jealous at the possibility of not being my solo client, other than my Uncle Bryan. He knows there's a serious connection between a client and his hairdresser. He above all my friends should know how serious our bond is.

"Twenty dollars," I say, walking back up the stairs. I may be pissed but never stupid when it comes to my money. And I bet Cedric won't lie about who hooked him up either.

"Bet. I'll check you tomorrow," he says before closing his window and leaving me and Rah alone. I can't believe that trick knows where my mom lives and had the nerve to step to me.

"I'll call you when I get home. I'm sorry about this girl, you have to know that." And the problem is that I know it all too well. We did solve some shit tonight and I know Trish will think twice about stepping to me the next time she wants to.

~ 8 ~
Down To The Root

"And time it turned/
He tried to burn me like a perm."

—LAURYN HILL/THE FUGEES

"**W**hat's got your panties in a bunch so early in the morning?" my mom says as she sips her coffee. I went to sleep before she got in last night but I know it was around two because she woke me up talking about it on the phone with her best friend, Vivica. Now she's dressed for a tennis match and ready to go. She must be having a lot of fun with Karl and I'm happy for her. She deserves a man who treats her like a queen.

"Oh, nothing much. I still can't believe I don't have to work this morning," I say, avoiding telling my mom about the loud argument between Rah, Trish, Tasha, and myself last night. I open the bare refrigerator, look around, and promptly close it. I guess I'll be making a run to the grocery market today.

"I know what you're thinking," she says only half-playing. If she set her mind to it, she'd hear me calling her a bad hostess for not having anything to eat in this house. She is my mother and I am visiting for the weekend, so where's the nourishment?

"I heard that," she says, sipping the last of her coffee. "And I know I should've stocked the kitchen but I've been too busy this week," my mom says as she adds the mug and spoon to the pile of dirty dishes in the sink. "Girl, I worked overtime every day to make up for all the days I've been taking off with Karl, but believe me it's been worth it." Her green eyes sparkle with joy every time she says his name. I guess I can't blame her for being happy. But do I have to suffer in the meantime?

"Mom, I'm feeling the love but you know I'm out of a job. I can't spend what little money I have on groceries." I take a tea bag out of the box on the counter and put it into a clean coffee mug. At least she's got hot water.

"Oh Jayd, stop being so overdramatic," she says, picking up her tennis bag from the floor by the dining room table. "You're not starving. There's Top Ramen and oatmeal. Work it out." My mom looks at me and I stare back at her, hoping to make her feel a little bit guilty. I would tell Mama on her but it won't help me get some food in my stomach this morning. My mom's eyes soften and she reaches into the side of her tennis bag and retrieves her wallet, pulling out a ten dollar bill and placing it on the table.

"Thank you," I say walking over to the table to claim the money before she changes her mind. I pick up the bill and tuck it into my purse, also sitting on the table and reminding me of Jeremy's declaration of love yesterday. Why did he have to ruin our relationship by attempting to buy my pride? And why does my guilt purse have to be so cute?

"You're welcome. Just make sure those dishes are clean when I get back." She takes her jacket off the couch and drapes it around her shoulders. She's going to be chilly when she steps out that door. But as she tells me too often, I'm not her mama even if the roles seem reversed at times.

"And when will that be?" I ask as she heads toward the front door. She looks stunning in a blue and white tennis dress with socks and shoes to match. Her matching Adidas jacket is also flyy—another gift from her new beau.

"Not sure, but I'll send you a text if I'm not going to make it home." She slings her bag over her shoulder, checks her purse for her keys, and opens the door, letting the morning cold in. She doesn't even shiver at the gust of air and I'm ready to jump back under the covers.

"Have fun and thanks again for the cash." Honestly, ten dollars is nothing with the price of food going up in Los Angeles County. But if I make some spaghetti and get a box of cereal and some milk, I should be cool until I get back to Mama's house tomorrow evening.

"I wish I could do more, Jayd. Enjoy your day," she says as she heads down the stairs. Before I can close the door, Cedric pokes his head out of his door, yelling up the stairs. "Hey Jayd, when can you hook my braids up?"

My mom looks back up and winks at me. *"We'll talk about your newfound profession later,"* my mom says from her mind to mine. *"And tell Rah I said hi.* Good morning, Cedric." Cedric looks at my mom walking down the driveway with his one good eye and almost forgets why he came out of his house at nine in the morning.

"Good morning, Lynn," he says. When she gets all the way down the driveway, Cedric walks up the stairs to talk to me. "Damn Jayd, your mama is fine. Do you think she likes younger dudes?" Like I'd ever hook him up with my mama. He must be smoking.

"In your dreams, Cedric," I say walking back into the house. My hair is wrapped up tight in a scarf and I still need to get dressed, although my oversize gray sweats and faded blue T-shirt are very comfortable. My comforter and sheets are still on the couch, my makeshift bed that suits me fine on the weekends.

"How'd you know?" he says, following me into the house. My mom gives him a few dollars here and there to run errands and wash her car from time to time. Cedric works the night shift at the Costco up the street and is usually home asleep during the day. "Don't be mad when you have to call me Daddy one day real soon."

"Whatever, fool. I can hook you up in a little while," I say, cleaning off the couch. "I need to do my own hair first." I stack my sleeping bag, comforter, and pillow on the floor next to the couch in front of the small closet where they really belong. I rarely bother putting them up until I leave on Sundays.

"What kind of customer service is that?" he says, leaning against the open front door. It's too early in the morning to be harassed. He's lucky I need the money. Otherwise I'd slam the door in his face and go back to bed.

"It'll be the kind where you don't get any service at all if you keep playing with me." My growling stomach makes me remember I'm also supposed to be walking to the market for breakfast. I don't know if I can make it that long. I would make some oatmeal but she doesn't have any milk, brown sugar, or butter, which are necessities as far as I'm concerned. Top Ramen's starting to sound real good.

"You a little hungry," he says, amused by my loud bodily functions. I ignore him and walk into the kitchen to check the cupboards for anything that will curb my appetite. I see the packages of chicken-flavored noodles and read the label of one, which expired over the summer. Damn, there goes that idea.

"Don't you have something better to do than harass me this early in the day?" My phone vibrates on the dining room table. I walk over to check who's calling and shoot Cedric an evil look. It's Rah. What's he doing up this early?

"Not really. You got something in mind?" I never take Cedric's proposals seriously but today I've got just the thing for him.

"Yes, I do," I say, writing on an empty envelope sitting on

the coffee table. "Here's a list of things I need from the store. By the time you get back I'll be ready to work. Make it happen." I pass him the list with the money my mom gave me and shove him out the door.

"Damn girl, are you serious? There's a lot of shit on this list." I can make a dollar stretch.

"Yes and I want my change. The sooner you get back the sooner you can get your hair braided. Now get." I should be able to get my hair done before he gets back if I work fast. I don't want to wait until the end of the day to do it because I may run out of steam. I'd rather accomplish my tasks early in the day and get them over with.

"Do I get gas money or something?" he says from behind the closed door. Gas is expensive and he is perpetually broke. I can't do him like that.

"Okay, you can keep the change," I yell as I grab my hair bag out of the hall closet and set up shop. A simple flat iron will do me good this morning. I'm not in the mood for anything too fancy. It feels good to be home on a Saturday and have the place to myself, even if I'm not quite alone yet.

"But that's only going to be about two dollars by the looks of what you've got on this list." I see he's good at pinching pennies too.

"Stop complaining. I've hooked you up plenty of times and you know you have to go to the store on a daily basis anyway to get your blunts or whatever. It's only up the street. How much gas can you burn?"

"You'll see when you get your own car. Then you'll know how a brotha feels." I can't wait to know how it feels to have my own car. I'll check my text message from Rah later. Right now I just want to wash this week out of my head. I doubt I'll attend the session tonight. The last thing I want is to watch Mickey and Nigel make out or have another run-in with one of Rah's girls. If I could figure out a way to help him out of this drama, I would do it in a heartbeat. But for now, we'll both have to deal with his mistakes.

It feels good to have a clean head. I like the way my hair feels soft and bouncy after a flat iron. When I've pressed it before, it's been much straighter and with less bounce. Jeremy liked it when I wore my hair like this the most. He said it was "aphrodisiactic" and I feel him. I feel like a princess when my crown is light like this. I can hear Cedric walking up the stairs with my groceries and open the door for him to come in. I finished my hair just in time.

"Hey, what y'all doing over there?" my mom's next-door neighbor Shawntrese says through her opened door. Cedric brings my groceries inside and takes them directly to the kitchen. Knowing my mom, he probably unpacks them for her too. But unlike her, I can handle the rest on my own.

"Nothing much. Just braiding Ced's hair this morning," I say, standing in the open door looking into her living room. Shawntrese also sleeps on the couch in her mother's apartment, where she's still perched from the night before.

"For real Jayd, you braiding now? Oh you've got to hook a sistah up!" Shawntrese removes her do-rag, revealing her tattered extensions. She does need the hookup but I'm afraid she requires more than I can do.

"I'm strictly cornrows, Shawntrese. No Korean or horsehair on my agenda." Shawntrese laughs at me and Cedric makes himself comfortable at the dining room table, where I've set up shop. "I could give you a press and curl if you take the rest of your braids out."

"Now that sounds like a plan. All I got on me is a twenty. Is that cool?" she says, naming my price before it comes out of my mouth. Mama's right about the power of thoughts. In a couple of hours I'll make what it would usually take me all day to make at Simply and I don't have to pay taxes. I could dig this lifestyle for real.

"That'll work, girl. I'll holla at you when I'm finished with Ced." As I close the door and prep my client's hair for parting, my cell vibrates with a message from Rah for the fifth time this morning. He keeps apologizing for Trish's behavior last night but I don't have much more to say to him. I'll help him when I can but right now I've got work to do, and it doesn't include making him feel better about his horrible choice in girlfriends or baby mamas.

"Damn Jayd, you can braid your ass off," Shawntrese says as I finish up the last of Cedric's braids. "Hurry up and move, fool, so she can get started on my hair." She's been here for the last five minutes and likes what she sees.

"You got a mirror?" Cedric says, rubbing his hands over his tightly woven scalp, pleased with the results before he even sets eyes on his fresh do.

"Here you go." I take the hand mirror out of my hair bag and pass it to him. "Did you put conditioner in your hair?" I say, rubbing my fingers through Shawntrese's wet tresses. She wears it in braids so much that her hairline has begun to recede and her hair is thinning. The perm in her hair isn't helping. Mama makes a fierce conditioner that can help her hair regain its natural strength and luster but I didn't bring any with me.

"No. I didn't have any left and my Mama hides her stuff from me. Ain't that cold?" she says, pushing a satisfied Cedric out of his seat, where she promptly sits down. She and her mother have a strange relationship.

"You need to work on your social skills, Shawntrese. Here you go, Jayd." Cedric hands me my payment with a smile on his face. "You've got a customer for life in me, shawty." I like making my clients happy. It's almost better than getting paid to do something that comes so naturally to me—almost.

"You're welcome. You know where to find me if you need a touch-up." I shake out the large towel before draping it across Shawntrese's shoulders. I'm going to need a spare one if I'm going to do other people's hair on a regular basis. Netta's very serious about mixing folks' hair together. She's says it can lead to confusing situations and I have enough confusion in my life as it is.

"Alright, clock's ticking. I've got a skate date tonight and I want to look good." Shawntrese is too funny. "And I want to know what all that noise was about last night. I would've come downstairs but I was too lit. I was listening from the balcony so I knew you had everything under control." I'm glad to know her being nosy is done out of concern.

"Yeah, you two girls go ahead and get your gossip on. I've got to get some sleep before I have to go to work in a few hours. Thanks again Jayd." Closing the door behind him, Cedric heads downstairs and lets me and Shawntrese catch up. We haven't talked since I witnessed the shooting a couple of months ago. And she stays with her boyfriend on most weekends so we rarely see each other when I'm here. Being here during the day is much more lively than I expected.

"You couldn't come help a sistah out last night," I say, plugging the blow dryer into the wall while Shawntrese makes herself comfortable. I place the dryer on the table and pick up the television remote control and hand it to her.

"Girl, I told you I was lit. Besides, my mama had company and I was trying to be as quiet as possible. I'm saving up my money now so I can get the hell out of here." Shawntrese is a few years older than me but she acts my age. I don't know if that's good or bad.

"I feel you there. I'm hustling hard for my car as you can see," I say, combing through her frail hair. The more I look at her scalp the more I'm sure I shouldn't put any stress on it. Heat would definitely damage her hair more than it already is.

"Yeah girl, you're on it. Doing hair is the way to go. If I had the patience I'd do it myself." She flips through the channels unaware of the issues I see in her head.

"Yeah, I like it much better than waiting on customers. Shawntrese, I know you have your heart set on a press and curl but I think we should try something else." I run my fingers through her hair, feeling her scalp and the pattern of her roots. At first I see cornrows all over her head, but that too might put more stress on her head than it can take. "How about I set tiny twists all over? It'll be much better for your hair, help it grow, and it'll look cute on your face." I pass the mirror to her in the hopes that she will see my vision.

"Are you sure?" she asks, looking at herself through my eyes. "I've never really rocked my hair out of braids or a perm." I rub my fingers quickly through her hair, twisting small sections so she can get a feel for what I'm talking about.

"Yeah, and that's your problem. You're killing your hair and I can't participate in the massacre," I say, throwing my hands up like I'm testifying in church. Shawntrese laughs at my dramatics and gets the point. "Trust me, I won't send you out looking crazy. I've got your back, even if you don't have mine," I say as I try to make her feel guilty for not coming outside last night.

"Jayd, that girl was on crutches and the other one was damn near a midget. I know you were cool and you can't tell me any differently. So spill it. What was that about?" I don't usually disclose my personal life to her but she's sitting in my chair so I'm obligated to spill a little.

"Rah's girl doesn't want me braiding his hair." Shawntrese stops staring at the television and turns her head to look up at me.

"What are you doing when you braid, girl? Should I be scared?" she says, holding her head in her hands. I smack her in the back of the head with a towel before draping her neck with it. What could I possibly do to someone while braiding his or her head?

"*A whole lot if you master that skill,*" my mom says, invading our conversation. "*You know Netta's got skills like Mama does when it comes to braiding hair. That's why they work so well together, even if they are nosy and controlling.*"

Mom, not now. I'm doing Shawntrese's hair, I think back. Shawntrese is now talking about the videos on the television. But while my mom's in my head, I can't concentrate on much else.

"*Oh girl, please. You can walk and chew bubble gum at the same time,*" my mom says, not leaving me alone. "*You need to study that part of your lessons tonight before you get too deep into doing other people's heads. You think Rah's girl is crazy for caring about you braiding his head but I know you know better.*"

"*How did you know about that?*" I ask, skillfully responding to Shawntrese's inquiries while simultaneously twisting up her hair. My mom's right: I can do two things at once.

"*Don't worry about all that. Take my advice Jayd. There are many things to consider before taking on this line of work, being a young priestess such as yourself. There's power in everything you do, especially this. You need to perform cleansings on your client and yourself before and after you do their hair and all kinds of other things you need to learn about. It's all in the book and Netta can help you apply it practically.*"

"Yeah, if she gives me the job. Mama doesn't seem to want me to have it."

"Well, Mama has her reasons but it's an unavoidable part of your path. Williams women were doing hair before we came to this country and got the last name Williams," my mom says. *"I feel like our ancestors who did hair on the plantation and that isn't a good feeling. You and Mama got the gift of our other ancestors who felt the power in it. I say embrace it, just be careful. Haters come in all walks of life. And make sure you don't leave hair all over my dining room."*

"Jayd, are you listening to me?" Shawntrese says, looking at me through the mirror. My mom leaves me to contemplate her words and finish my job. I have a lot of work to do tonight, which is perfect. All I feel like doing is curling up on the couch and chilling. I'll send Rah a quick text to let him know he won't be seeing me at the session this evening. I've got to focus on my lineage if I'm going to help anyone out, including myself.

"Yeah girl, I hear you," I say, wiping the aloe vera gel mixture I make especially for natural hairstyles like this one off my hands and onto her towel. "Let me send this message while I'm thinking about it and then I'm all yours." I grab my cell from the table and locate Rah's last message, hitting reply.

I've got a lot of studying to do, Rah. I'll check you in the morning. Peace.

"So like I was saying, do you think Beyoncé's prettier with short hair or long hair?" Shawntrese says, eyeing her transition in the video on BET. "I like the weave but she's rocking it cut too."

"I like the lyrics. She's singing my feelings right now," I say as I sing along to "Me, Myself and I" while Shawntrese joins in. Rah responds to my message instantly. I don't want to go back and forth with him all day but I do want to know how he's feeling. I've already got gel on my hands so my client will have to help me out.

"Can you check my phone please?" I ask Shawntrese, who gladly grabs the buzzing cell off the table.

"It says, 'You can't avoid me forever. I'll see you tomorrow afternoon to take you home. I love you girl.' You've got this boy sprung, girl. Are you sure you're still a virgin?"

"Yes, and as crazy as these girls and boys are out here, I'm staying this way for a long, long time." It's bad enough the mental games get us into our fair share of drama, but the physical ramifications of messing with the wrong person are also too much for me to deal with. I'd hate to be in Mickey's, Tania's, and Sandy's shoes right now. All of their problems have one element in common: getting caught up because they had sex with the wrong dude. I'm staying on this side of that rope for as long as I can.

~ 9 ~

Let It Burn

"Let it burn, let it burn, let it burn."

—USHER

After Shawntrese leaves, I clean up the dining room and start dinner while watching this old white man on PBS talk about following certain laws to attract goodness in life. He makes it sound like a guaranteed formula that will work for anyone. If life were that easy people wouldn't need to come to Mama for help. Jeremy called again but I didn't answer—again. I don't know what else to say to him. The bottom line is that even though it hurts like hell, no matter how much we want to be more than friends, we can't. And the sooner we both realize it, the better off we'll both be.

My mom left her spirit notebook out for me to look at. I thought she'd never let me see it again after I gave it back to her a couple of weeks ago. I got one tiny chocolate stain on the back cover and she freaked out. For someone who doesn't care much about her lessons from Mama, she sure is protective of that book.

My mom has notes of a tea that she used on an ex-boyfriend that kept his other broads away from him. I think I should look this up tomorrow when I get back to Mama's. But the notes my mom has here are pretty good too. As much drama as Rah's had lately, I'm sure he'll want to take a sip of this tea. I'll make it for him tomorrow when he takes me home. Until then, I'm going to chill and enjoy my time alone, a treat I very rarely get.

Rah felt really bad about me having to deal with Trish and Sandy the night before and decided to give me a ride to Mama's today and I'm glad. I studied the concoction in my mom's journal and it doesn't seem hard to make. It says that when they come too close to his scent they'll be repelled. Sounds good to me. Now I just have to get him to be in agreement with me and we're good to go.

"Jayd, are you sure your grandmother doesn't mind us being back here?" Rah says as we walk into the spirit room behind a possessive Lexi, who's sniffing him down. Recognizing his smell, she retreats to the corner for a late afternoon nap so we can get to work. Hopefully we'll be in and out before Mama gets home.

"You know Mama has a soft spot for you," I say, directing him to put my bags under the table and sit down on one of the wooden stools. "Besides, she's not back here so it's all good." I just want to make Rah his tea and get out of here before she finds out what I'm up to. Even if Rah has given me permission to help him, I don't think Mama wants me helping anyone else until I get myself together first. But part of my getting together is getting Rah together, though somehow I don't think Mama would see it my way.

"So what are you making me? Is it going to taste good?" he asks, watching me look through the large book on the table. I turn to the back to a section entitled "Tinctures and Teas." I thumb through the pages and find a recipe similar to the one in my mom's notebook. I copied down her notes into mine to compare the ingredients on each list.

"Yes, I think it is. And it's a tea to help you not smell irresistible to anyone but me." I take the antique teapot off the tiny stove and fill it up in the sink. The recipe is pretty basic except for one special herb I've never used before. "Can you look in the cabinet and hand me a coffee mug?"

"Sure thing, Queen Jayd," he says, smiling at me as he reaches into the cabinet behind his head. The door almost hits him in the face when he opens it due to the tight space. Whenever someone other than Mama and myself are in here, the room feels smaller than usual.

"Thank you." I take the mug from Rah and place the tiny round tea infuser inside. According to the directions, I'm supposed to stuff the ingredients into the infuser and pour the boiling water over it. If I want to be resistant to the effects I have to take a sip too. For both our sakes, I hope it tastes better than it sounds. "Now for the fun part."

"I don't like the way you said that," he says, watching me closely. "You're not still mad at me are you?"

"That's a good question to ask someone who's about to feed you. But no, I'm not mad at the fact that you can't handle your business like a man." Rah looks sad as my words hit the air and I realize I've hurt his feelings. "You're in my prayers." I reach across the table to squeeze his cheeks, but he only looks slightly amused.

"Yeah, I just hope they're good prayers." I know he's only joking but it stings a little for him to think that I would wish harm on anyone, especially him. Ever since my trying to help Misty blew up in my face, everyone's been acting a little distant in their own way, including Rah. I know they can't help it. My friends need time to adjust to learning about my heritage, but Rah has always known what's up with me.

"What do you mean by that?" I ask, gathering teaspoons of ingredients from the various glass canisters lining the shelves. Everything's in alphabetical order, making it easy to locate the tools I need for the "Bitter Bwoy Brew" I'm making.

"Nothing, girl. Don't go getting all sensitive on me now. You know I'm just joking, right?" The teapot whistles loudly and I turn it off. Mama's yellow sunflower oven mitt fits my hand perfectly, allowing me to pick up the hot pot and pour the boiling water over the concoction. The steam overwhelms my face, almost burning me, but it still feels good. I hope the brew is as potent as it smells. After waiting for the drink to cool, it's finally ready.

"Here, have some tea." I take a sip with my teaspoon before passing the bitter elixir to Rah. He takes the warm mug and hesitates slightly before drinking it down in three swift gulps. Now that's true faith in me. I know he trusts me but sometimes I wonder how much.

"Good boy. Now you'll be all better," I say, patting Rah's hand like Mama does me. He scrunches up his face like he's in some serious pain. I guess the bitter herbs are finally reaching his taste buds. From the looks of it, the aftertaste must be worse than actually drinking the strong tea.

"What the hell was in that shit? That was awful," he says, grabbing a paper towel from the roll on the table and wiping his mouth. If he were at home he'd probably try and scrub his tongue with it. He glares at me as I laugh at his reaction while cleaning up my mess. The sun is beginning to set and we both need to get ready for our school week. I'm glad we only have three days of school with Thanksgiving—or misgiving holiday as Mama calls it—this Thursday. It makes the time more palatable.

"It has to be bitter to work. It did smell kind of raunchy though." I squeeze more Palmolive onto the yellow sponge as I continue my cleaning. "I'll make you something sweet to make up for it next weekend, promise." Rah rises from the kitchen table and puts the towel down on the counter beside the sink. He steps behind me as I wash the dishes, putting his arms around my waist. He could never smell bad to me; I don't care what kind of potion he takes. I hope the same isn't true for Trish and Sandy.

"You're all the sweet I need," he says, kissing the side of my neck and sending shivers down my belly. Rah gets a rise out of me like no other dude ever has. Jeremy's the closest but even he had his limitations. I could stay wrapped up in Rah's arms indefinitely. "Thank you for helping me, Jayd, for real."

"You're welcome." I pick up another towel hanging from the rack above the sink and dry my hands. "Okay, that's enough touching. I've got to get inside and you need to get going. The rats come out at night, remember." I turn around to face Rah, still enclosed in his tight grip. He kisses me soft and slow at first, tasting every bit of the tea remnants lingering on my lips. I give into the moment, wrapping my arms around his neck and allowing him to pull me in closer to him. I know I'm going to suffer more hurt with Rah but I can't help my strong feelings for him. I just hope I'll be able to always keep us safe from the haters.

After Rah leaves, I join Mama in the kitchen and catch up with her about our weekends. She apparently got home a few minutes ago and had a taste for something sweet. And I'm glad she did because she's making my favorite dessert.

"Honey cakes have been in our family for generations, Jayd. Even your mother can make these well," she says as she mixes the golden batter counterclockwise in the large glass bowl.

"Yeah, when she has to," I say, adding vanilla to the mix. The smell hits my nose, instantly making me hungry for a taste. I swirl my index finger in the batter and take a scoop to sample.

"Jayd, what have I told you about putting your finger in my food, girl?" Mama says, tapping me on the hand with the wooden spoon and unintentionally rewarding me with more to taste.

"Mmm, thank you." I lick the rest of the batter off my fingers before washing them in the sink. "These cakes are going to be good."

"Yes, they are. So how was your weekend?" she asks as she drops spoonfuls of her sweet creation onto the cookie sheet covered in parchment paper. They're the size of cookies and as soft as cakes after they bake.

"It was cool. I made some money and that's always good," I say, sitting down across from her at the kitchen table. Mama's still dressed and looks ready to peel off her long day.

"Legally, I hope?" I know Mama's joking but she does worry about us getting caught up in the streets. The last thing I would ever do is something that'll get me put in jail or killed. If I did, the punishment I'd suffer from Mama would be worse than death.

"Yes, Mama. I had three hair clients and made as much in a few hours as I would have working all weekend at the restaurant." Mama watches me tell her my news and her eyes shimmer with interest. Is she happy that I found my new hustle or listening for something else I'm not consciously saying? "Which reminds me, has Netta said anything about me working with her?"

"I'm not so sure about that," she says, leaning back in her chair and crossing her arms over her chest. Big breasts run in our lineage, just like our other gifts. "You know it's not an ordinary hair shop, Jayd. You can't bring trouble to our haven." Contrary to popular belief, I don't like drama even if it does seem to follow me wherever I go.

"I understand that, Mama, and that's why I want to work there." I'm going to plead my case until she reconsiders. "I've been thinking about this for a while now and I think it would be really good for my spirit studies too. Besides, this way you could keep an even closer eye on me." Mama leans her head to one side, looking at me in disbelief.

"Jayd, you're good but you're not that good," Mama says,

rising from her seat to check on the cakes. "Oh shit, didn't you smell them burning?" she says, taking the hot sheet out of the oven. Mama's been complaining about that stove for over a year now and Daddy still hasn't taken care of it. Mama's determined to buy a new one with her own money, which will take a while to save up. She charges almost nothing for her services and volunteers whenever she works outside of the house. If I could get her a new stove I would.

"I'm sorry, Mama." I don't know why I'm apologizing. She was as close to the stove as I was and her nose works way better than mine. I guess she's feeling a bit off today. Ever since my uncles had it out again and Esmeralda's been on my case, Mama hasn't looked well.

"Don't talk back to your grandmother, not even in your own head," my mother intrudes. *"She may not be able to read your mind like I can but she knows what you're thinking, Jayd. Trust me on this one."* Mama looks up from her overbrowned treats and smiles at me.

"Listen to your mother, Jayd. Remember she's already been down this path with me before. And tell her she needs to get over here for a reading or else I'm coming to her house." I know my mom doesn't want that. The last time Mama went over to her house she did a cleansing and smudged the entire building with sage, drawing more attention from the neighbors than my mother wants.

"Ah hell nah, she can't come over here. Tell her I'll see her after the holiday. I'm out. See you Wednesday, baby." I'm glad I get to go to my mom's house for holidays. The more time I can spend away from the men in this house, the better.

"She says after Thanksgiving," I say standing behind Mama, ready to sample the sweets. Personally, I like my cookies a little burnt. "What did my mom mean that you can tell what I'm thinking?" I wait for her to pass me a cookie.

"Oh Jayd, why do you ask questions you already know the

answer to? Besides, I can't tell you everything. Some things you need to learn about on your own." Now Mama looks deeply contemplative. After a few moments of silence and Mama picking at the delicate treats, I decide to ask for one. But before I can, she instinctively passes me one and piles the rest in a stack on the warm sheet.

"No matter how they may look, these are the bomb, Mama." I devour the tasty treat in two bites. They're so soft and moist they could melt in my mouth.

"Slow down, Jayd. That's always been one of your major problems, girl. You move too damn fast." I look into Mama's eyes and can tell she's talking about way more than me and my fetish for honey cakes. "I saw Rah's car out front when I got home. How come he didn't come in to say hello?"

"He had to pick up Kamal from his grandmother's house and he was already running late." I was hoping Mama wouldn't pick up on that but who am I kidding? Mama picks up on everything.

"Do you know why I burnt these cakes, Jayd?" she says as she picks through the pile of cookies and tosses out the burnt ones. There are only three dozen and she's already thrown away seven of them. Part of me wants to take them out of the trash but I know Mama would trip on me for something like that.

"I know, Mama. It was my fault. I should've smelt them burning," I say, watching her toss more into the bin. Maybe I can get them out when she goes to her room.

"No. Because my emotions got the best of me. And as with all practitioners, you must separate your emotions from your work. Otherwise, you get caught up in the desired outcome and can hurt yourself in the process. My senses were off because I was worried about your uncles and your stupid grandfather when I should have been concentrating on my work," she says, putting the least burnt ones in a Ziploc bag before leading the way to our room. "Just be careful, Jayd. That's the third rule: don't get emotionally attached to your work. It'll cloud your vision and we as Williams women can never be off when it comes to our sight."

"Mama, do you ever think of what we do as magic?" I ask as I lay across my bed and Mama sits on hers, placing the bag on the nightstand between our twin beds. Mama looks exhausted. I know she's had a long weekend helping the homeless shelter on Rosecrans prepare their annual Thanksgiving dinner. Mama chairs the event and has done so since I can remember. Daddy and my uncles and Jay have dinner at the church with the rest of the church members, which includes half the block. I usually kick it at my mom's and go wherever she goes, unless she has a date. Then I'm alone and that doesn't bother me one bit.

"Jayd, doing hair for people is the same as making food for them. It's all nourishment and you must have people's trust in order to be effective. There's nothing like doing someone's hair and making him or her feel like a different person." She rubs her feet with the menthol and shea butter cream she made a few days ago.

"How do we nourish through doing hair?" If that's what I've been doing all weekend then I should've charged my clients double. I'll remember that when I meet new clients. Mama pauses before answering me. She doesn't want me to take my newfound career lightly.

"There's a story about Oshune helping Orunmilla—the prophet of our religion—and how Legba facilitated this by having Orunmilla pour cold water on her head every day until she gives in to Orunmilla's demands." Mama stretches her legs out on her bed and relaxes a bit. I know she wants to get out of her dress and panty hose, but she looks too tired to move anymore.

"Mama, everything I know about Oshune says she's a strong warrior woman who can't be moved unless she wants to be." Mama laughs at my interpretation of our deity but nods her head in agreement.

"Yes Jayd, it is true that Oshune can be stubborn. But we all need help and it starts with a cool head. She agreed because Orunmilla was messing with her head thereby creating chaos in her daily life." I remember Netta telling me how Mama was so powerful as a hairdresser that people accused her of messing with their heads back in New Orleans. Mama was hurt by the accusations and still feels the pain.

"So why didn't she use some of her other powers to get rid of them both?" She looks at me, searching for some recognition of the right answer in my eyes but it's not coming. After several minutes of quiet, Mama gives me my final lesson for the night.

"Peace of mind starts with a clean head and it's more precious than most people give it credit for, Jayd. Remember, it's the head that carries the body that moves the feet. The whole point is conserving the power in your crown. Doing hair is another powerful and envious part of our lineage. You can ask Netta about the job yourself when you meet me there on Tuesday with your protection potion in hand."

"Oh Mama, thank you," I say reaching across the small space between our beds and hugging her tightly. "I promise I won't let y'all down."

"I know, Jayd. Just be careful and listen to Netta and me when we tell you to do something. And try not to ask too many questions when we do. Trust is the first step in any relationship, especially between a student and her teachers."

Exactly. I'm learning to trust Rah more and more as he opens himself up to trusting me completely. I hope the tea works. I guess I'll have to wait to find out when he goes to school tomorrow. I hope it takes. I've had better luck with making food than gris-gris, so I'm pretty confident in my abilities.

"What's Misty doing at my house again?" I say to myself as I walk into the living room to see Mama having tea with my sworn enemy. They're using Mama's good china that she reserves for feeding the Orisha. Has she lost her mind?

"Oh hello Jayd. You're just in time for some tea," Mama says, pouring me a cup though I'm too confused to drink anything. Misty looks up from her cup but her eyes don't belong to her: they're a shade of green I've never seen before. She picks up the honey sitting on the serving tray and takes a spoonful, putting it in my cup. I take a seat in the rocking chair across from the couch where they are seated, as directed by Mama. But her eyes look different, making me feel like I should stay on my guard just in case I have to make a move for the door.

"Jayd don't be rude. Have a sip," Mama says as she picks up the saucer and cup from the coffee table and forces me to take it. "Misty made it just for you." I really don't want it. I can't trust Misty as far as I can throw her and she's a thick sistah.

"Yeah Jayd. I'd thought I'd return the favor. I'm trying to help you like you tried to help me by making that gris-gris," she says pushing the cup toward my mouth. But I resist. I don't care if it is a dream. I'll be damned if I take anything that trick gives me; I don't care if Mama was there when she made it.

"No thank you. I appreciate the gesture but really, I'm good." I stand up and head for the back door, ready to retreat to the backhouse. Before I can turn around and leave the two to their twisted teatime, Misty thrusts the cup at me again, spilling the hot concoction all over me.

"Ahhh," I scream as the steaming liquid burns my skin. It

feels hotter than any tea I've ever known and my skin is itching like crazy. What the hell?

"Jayd, get up before you're late," Mama says. My skin is still itching from my dream. I need to work on something to help me control my dreams, for real.

"I'm up Mama." I pull back my blankets and let in the cold morning air.

"And don't forget to get started on your potion if you haven't already. Remember, you're meeting with Netta tomorrow." Mama's on point for someone who's barely awake. I wonder if the potion will protect me in my dream world too.

"Okay Mama." I'm anxious to talk with Netta tomorrow about my new position. I only hope she's as excited as I am. I can't wait to get through this school day just so I can get to tomorrow. Too bad Mondays have to come first.

I'm hoping to start off my school week with a little less drama than last week. Mainly I was hoping that I would wake up and realize that Mickey really wasn't pregnant with God only knows whose baby. I've got to convince her to come clean and keep Nellie from blowing her cover at the same time. Sometimes having more than one homegirl is highly overrated.

Jeremy didn't come for me at the bus stop this morning but I did get a text from him saying he was running late and was sorry he would miss me. Rah also texted me to say good morning and that his mouth was still burning from the tea. I hope that's a good thing.

"So what's up with you this morning?" Mickey says as I follow her into the girl's bathroom in the main hall. Nellie had to meet with the other ASB members to help with the canned food drive on Wednesday, which is a joke because Nellie doesn't have a charitable bone in her body. But as a crowned princess she has to work with the rest of the court.

Mickey walks through the door and automatically looks under the stalls, checking for feet. "There's someone in here with us." Instead of hiding, this time Misty opens her stall door and steps out. I would say something smart to her but she looks like crap. I'm trying to be obedient and stay out of Misty's business but something tells me not to. I feel for the girl even if she did creep her way into my dream this morning. Mickey on the other hand could care less about her and now's the perfect time for her to exercise revenge.

"Well, look what crawled out of the toilet," Mickey says, turning away from the mirror and walking toward Misty, who's holding her stomach like I hold mine when I cramp. I hope she's not on her period because Mickey's about to bite into her no matter what time of the month it may be.

"I wasn't listening to the two of you bitch," Misty says as she steps around Mickey to wash her hands at the sinks. When Misty sets her purse on the counter she notices it's wet and reaches for a paper towel to wipe the counter before setting the bag on it.

"If I weren't pregnant I'd mop the floor with your curly bush of a head," Mickey says, stepping behind Misty and forcing her to look at her in the mirror's reflection. Mickey's much taller than Misty and even more intimidating, which makes Misty nervous.

"Mickey, let's get going before the bell rings." I'm trying to diffuse the situation. I don't want to witness Mickey bully Misty even if she does deserve it for trying to rat out Mickey's pregnancy to Nigel. If Misty knew that the paternity was in question I'm sure she'd spread that around school as quickly as possible too.

"Oh come on, Jayd. I'm just having fun." Mickey flicks Misty's long hair with her claw-like acrylic nails. The look on Misty's face tells me she's in pain and Mickey's scaring the hell out of her. It reminds me of how I felt in my dream about Misty this morning. I just wanted to be left alone and they kept pressuring me, eventually causing me to get burned. Maybe the dream wasn't about me as much as it was about Misty.

"Okay Wolverine, let's go." I grab my girl by the arm, but not before she lets go of Misty's hair.

"Ouch," Misty says, instinctively holding her head with both hands and causing her purse and its contents to crash to the floor. The gris-gris bag I made for her slides across the floor, landing in front of my feet. Why is she still carrying this around? After all I went through because of her fear of it, now she's using it as a charm?

"Well, what do we have here?" Mickey follows Misty's eyes away from my feet and toward the pill bottle near the bathroom door. Misty reaches for the bottle first but Mickey swoops it up before she can get to it. "Gonorrhea! Oh this is too good to be true," Mickey says, as she laughs her way out of the bathroom and into the busy hall.

"Give that back Mickey! I need my medicine," Misty shouts after her, running ahead of me but I'm right behind them both. Mickey stops, turns around, throws the bottle at Misty's feet. Instead of me being the one getting burnt, this time it's definitely Misty.

"I don't need it anyway. The proof is in the pudding, or in this case your cookies, which are stank and everybody's about to find out just how stank they really are." Mickey turns on her heels and speeds down the busy hall. Misty picks up the bottle of pills and looks back at me like it's all my fault. I wish I could stop Mickey from spreading the news but I know she's not going to hear me. Misty will have to deal with her consequences, both physical and social. And from the looks of it, they'll probably be equally excruciating.

~ 10 ~
Hot Air

"Nothing can save you/
For this is the season of catching the vapors."

—BIZ MARKIE

The scariest thing about having dreams that always come true in one way or another is seeing them play out once I'm awake. I never wished anything bad on Misty—not even after she led the witch hunt against me for making the same charm she's now carrying around in her purse. All that heat she gave me for leaving it for her was nothing but a bunch of steam to front for I don't know what. Now I'm sure she's wishing she'd heeded my initial assistance; maybe I would've dreamt a different dream.

The crowd is out on the quad today, even if it is only sixty degrees. In southern California that's damn near freezing. But the sun is bright and the vibe's relaxed, at least for the time being. I didn't want to leave Misty in the main hall like that but my girl's about to spread all of Misty's business and it's more important for me to stop her before it's too late.

"Mickey, don't do this. I'm telling you it's not going to end well," I say, following behind my girl, who can't get to South Central quick enough. She's not hearing me at all. All Mickey sees is red and Misty is in for all her rage.

"Why are you protecting her, Jayd? She doesn't give a damn about you," Mickey shouts over her shoulder, continuing her marathon through the quad. We have barely two minutes left before the bell rings and I don't want to be late for government class. Nigel, Chance, and Jeremy are sitting on the benches directly across from where KJ, his boys, Shae, Tony, and the rest of South Central are chilling. Maggie and her crew are also chilling in El Barrio, the area where the Latino brothers and sisters mainly chill. Everyone is out to witness Mickey's lethal announcement except for Misty, but I'm sure she'll be here soon enough.

"I'm not protecting her. It's you I'm worried about." Mickey stops in her tracks and faces me. I don't know if I can win her compassion but it's worth a shot.

"What are you talking about? Only good can come of me letting everyone know just how foul Misty is—literally," Mickey puts her right hand on her hip and looks down at me. I almost feel like I'm the one whose mind is being swayed.

"Mickey, think about the consequences. If you tell the entire school that Misty has an STD, she'll be unfairly judged when the one we should be looking at is KJ." Mickey rolls her eyes at me like I do when Mama's not looking. She knows I'm right about this. Girls are always judged more harshly than dudes when it comes to anything sexual. For a girl to brand another girl dirty is against all the rules and can only breed more disaster, especially where Misty's concerned.

"I don't give a damn about either one of them. And as far as consequences, I don't have anything to hide." How can Mickey stand there and lie to me and to herself? Has she forgotten Misty lives in Compton just like we do? Although Mickey and her man live on one side of the railroad tracks and me and Misty live on the other, it's a very small city and drama travels fast.

"Are you sure about that Mickey? You don't have anything to hide?" I ask. Her eyes turn cold as she gets my drift. It doesn't take a brain surgeon to figure out that her baby could be either her man's or Nigel's and Misty probably already has

her doubts. If Mickey does this to her I'm sure Misty will retaliate in the worst way she can think of and I'm certain it'll
have something to do with Mickey's man.

"I'm not afraid of Misty and I don't have a real problem
with KJ. But if it makes you feel better I'll call them both out.
How about that?" she says, turning back around in hot pur-
suit of her target. I think I just made matters worse. Why did
this have to happen right before third period? I can't afford
another tardy in Mrs. Peterson's class.

"Hey baby," Mickey says, kissing Nigel on the lips before
walking up to KJ's table. Jeremy and Chance look at me and
from my expression they know something's up.

"What's Mickey going over there for?" Nigel asks, eating
the last of his soft pretzel and mustard. "Did KJ say something about the game on Sunday to y'all?" If Nigel only knew
how over his head the situation really is. Their basketball
game is the last thing on Mickey's mind.

"No Nigel, it's not that." I stop at their table and watch the
scene unfold with the rest of them. "Mickey found out something about Misty and KJ and she's about to spill the beans."

"It's probably something like that nigga gave her the clap,
huh Jayd?" How did Nigel get that dead on? Reading into my
silence, the boys look at each other in recognition of the secret. "Damn, that's heavy." And Mickey's about to let everyone else know the truth, even if it's not her truth to tell.
Clapping as she stands in front of KJ's face, my girl begins
her exposé.

"Congratulations, KJ. I heard the good news," she says,
clapping obnoxiously in his face. KJ backs away from Mickey
and looks at her like she's gone mad.

"The hormones already getting to your head, huh?" KJ says
as he and his boys laugh. Mickey laughs with them, catching
them all off-guard. Her applause grows louder, getting the
group's attention.

"Oh, you are so funny, KJ," Mickey says, pretending to laugh harder than necessary. "You're right. The pregnancy has made me a little sensitive so I better back up from you if I want to stay clean. We all know what happened to Misty after she got too close, don't we?" she says, slowly clapping and allowing the reality to settle into KJ's brain. He looks at her like he wants to punch her in the face. Noticing the vibe shift, Nigel jumps up to defend his woman.

"Mickey, what's the problem?" Nigel asks. Chance, Jeremy, and I follow Nigel just as Misty comes out of the main hall, headed our way.

"Shut your girl up before she goes too far, man," KJ says, rising to meet Nigel's eyes. Looking past us, Mickey notices Misty's approach and decides to meet her halfway.

"Misty, come tell everyone the good news," she says, clapping the entire way there. Even Laura, Reid, and Nellie look up from their worktable to witness the festivities. Noticing my panic, Nellie decides to intervene for all our sakes.

"Mickey, what's going on?" Nellie says, falling in step with our girl gone wild. Not slowing down, Mickey entertains Nellie's questions and her plan.

"I'm going to let the entire school know that Misty and KJ have the clap. Care to watch?"

"Gonorrhea," Nellie whispers to Mickey but we can still hear her. We are only a step behind her but it feels like Mickey's miles away and determined to take Misty with her.

"Do you know another kind of clap?" Mickey teases, looking at Nellie out the side of her eyes before stopping Misty in her tracks. As usual, no one has Misty's back, not even the dude who gave her the STD. All KJ cares about is himself.

"Well, if you ask me this is not the way to handle it," Nellie says. "If you do this you'll be no better than Misty. Is that what you really want?" I hope Nellie takes her own advice when it comes to airing Mickey's dirty laundry to Nigel or her man.

"I don't recall asking your opinion about shit, Nellie. Why don't you go back over there with the rest of the squares and let me do my thing." I see the hurt on Nellie's face and know Mickey's in for the rudest surprise of all. How did this situation spin out of control so quickly?

"Karma's a bitch, Mickey, and so are you," Nellie says, passing us up to get back to the ASB table with the rest of the popular crew. "Good luck saving her from herself, Jayd." Ignoring both our warnings, Mickey continues with her parade as the warning bell rings above our heads. I shouldn't even stay. But like everyone else, I'm glued to my spot.

"How are you feeling, Misty? You and KJ should really take a sick day or maybe two," Mickey says. Misty looks like a deer caught in a trap: completely helpless. KJ steps in between the two of them, trying to silence Mickey, but he's too late. "How long does it take for gonorrhea to clear up?" Saying it loud enough for anyone walking past us headed for class to hear, Mickey allows the bombshell to drop from her mouth, sending a wave of shock through the crowd.

"Damn nigga, she gave you the clap," Del says to his boy while he and C Money look at a mortified Misty in disgust. Tears begin to fall down Misty's rosy cheeks as the whispers begin. It'll take her a long time to live this one down.

"You should always cover up your little soldier man, especially with girls you ain't really with, dog," C Money says. Shae, Tony, and the rest of their crew laugh at the situation while my boys and me look as sorry for Misty as she feels. Like I said before, when you sleep with the wrong people you will get burned one way or another. Unfortunately for Misty, her foul attitude has come back to bite her in the ass and we were all here to witness it.

"What's wrong, Misty? I've never seen you speechless before," Mickey says, still antagonizing her prey. Mickey can be real mean when she wants to be.

"Come on, Mickey, that's enough," Nigel says, taking her by the arm and leading her away from the scene. "We'll catch up with y'all later."

"Alright man," Chance says as he and Jeremy look at me looking at Misty. I feel terrible but even if I did try to help her she wouldn't let me. Too bad she has no real friends at school.

"Come on, Jayd. We'd better get to the office and get a late pass to class." Jeremy's right. Mrs. Peterson's going to have a field day with us being tardy again but I'm much more concerned about Misty's retaliation. Her taking it out on Mickey means taking it out on me too.

"Misty, do you want us to walk you to class?" I ask, not able to help myself from wanting to help her. She doesn't answer but looks up at me instead and I notice a shift in her eyes. Instead of being red and swollen from crying they are now cold and hard. She doesn't even look like herself anymore, just like her and Mama in my dream. I don't like this feeling at all. I'm going to have to get some feedback from Mama about this one but it will have to wait until tomorrow at Netta's. Mama's working at the shelter all week in the evenings, leaving us very little time to chat.

"Whoever said I had it?" KJ yells loud enough for everyone to hear. I know he's lying to save face but his word is bond to these followers around here, unlike Misty's word. And that's the problem with boys, especially the popular cats like him: they can get away with this shit, leaving the girls to take all the blame. I'm glad I had enough sense to protect my cookies from this monster. My phone vibrates, indicating a text from Rah. I hope it's good news about the tea. If it is I'm getting right on another amulet for Misty while I work on my protection potion tonight, now that I know she actually wants my help. I'm sure there have to be exceptions for people who want our help but can't ask for it. No girl should have to go through this type of humiliation alone and I'm sure Mama would agree.

When I got home I went straight to the spirit room until it was time for bed. Mama spent all day working at the shelter and she also turned in early last night. Rah and I spoke briefly, filling each other in on our days. Unfortunately he didn't get to test the tea because Trish didn't come to school yesterday and he hasn't seen Sandy yet, but I'm sure she'll pop up. I hope there's no expiration date on the tea taking effect. I also created a sweet-smelling oil as my protection potion and named it "drama repellent." We'll see how this works when I show it to Mama later at the shop. Until I figure out a way to help out my girls and Misty, I'm staying to myself, and I hope this repellent does its job well.

Noticing me on the bus this morning, Misty turns her head toward the window and pretends not to know me. Normally that would be okay with me, but this morning I feel obligated to speak. Not because I want to be friends with her but to let her know that I don't think she's nasty because she caught an STD. I already thought badly of her. I do, however, think the situation is wrong and that she's getting the raw end of the deal.

"What's up, Misty?" I say as I pass by her seat on my way to the back of the bus. It's crowded and my usual seat at the front is occupied. She doesn't move an inch or even attempt to acknowledge my greeting. Whatever, I tried. As I take a seat across from the row behind her the bus pulls off. The ride from Compton to Gardena is the longest ride of the three buses I take every day. As I settle in for the journey, Misty turns around in her seat and glares at me. Her eyes are just as cold as they were yesterday and in my dream. What the hell?

"You did this to me," Misty whispers in a cryptic voice. If I didn't know better I'd say the girl was possessed by a demon or something. She's really gone off the deep end this time if she thinks I gave her gonorrhea.

"Come again," I say, pulling out my phone so I can text my boo on the way to school. Rah's probably not even awake yet but I need a distraction from this trick and reading won't do. Where's my repellent? Maybe I need to put on some more oil because this girl is drama central.

"I know you did this to me for telling everyone your dirty little secret."

"First of all my secret wasn't dirty or little. And even if I did want to get back at you, I didn't give you a sexually trans- mitted disease, emphasis on the word 'sexually.' We were close, Misty, but never that close," I respond, turning away from her and looking out my own window. I search my purse for the small vial of the pink potion to rub all over myself be- cause the small amount I put on after my morning shower isn't helping now. Misty looks at me like I'm her worst enemy when she should be focusing all of her hatred on KJ.

"Well then, how do you explain me catching gonorrhea when the only guy I've ever been with is clean? I know you put a spell on me or something, Jayd." Did I just hear her right? She really thinks that KJ's creeping ass isn't the culprit?

"Oh come on, Misty," I say, spinning my head around in disbelief. "Even you can't be that gullible." But from the ex- pression on her face, she is. "KJ's lying to you and you're stu- pid enough to take the blame. Oh no, wait. You're stupid enough to blame me." This is too much for me this early in the morning. We still have a good half hour left on this ride and I don't want to spend it arguing with her.

"I knew I should've thrown away that evil charm bag but I was too afraid. And now look what you've done to me," she says, throwing the gris-gris at me. I never thought about what to do with it if someone doesn't want it. I'll have to ask Mama about that later. Right now I have to get her to shut up once and for all.

"Misty, if I really am the one causing the plagues on your ass then do you think it's smart to throw shit at me?" I don't mean to use my spiritual lineage to instill fear but the potion ain't working and I need some peace. I pick up the small charm bag from my lap and put it into my purse along with my oil. Misty backs off for right now but I know she's already planning her revenge. Hopefully, Mama can give me some pointers on how to make the potion strong enough to repel Misty. Until then, intimidation will have to do. She thinks I'm to blame for her cookies crumbling and that can only mean she's reached a point of total desperation and a desperate Misty is a dangerous thing.

I managed to avoid Misty and her drama as well as my girls and theirs for the rest of the day. Nellie's busy with her ASB duties and Mickey's busy keeping Nigel wrapped up in their instant family world. What I'd give for a day with no issues to dodge.

When I get to Netta's shop, the first thing we discuss is Misty's ridiculous accusations against me. It's bad enough she thinks I'm trying to harm her, but spreading her nonsense around school and the neighborhood just can't happen anymore. The girl has gone too far with this one and I have a feeling it's going to go even further if I don't check her ass immediately.

"You need to treat Misty like air Jayd. You know she's there but you don't see or hear her." Mama's on point with that one. There's nothing like talking to Mama and Netta at the same time. It's like getting two different yet equally powerful bits of wisdom about any topic. And banishing Misty and her crazy family is one of their favorites.

"That's probably how that child got her name. They knew she was going to be a hot air dispenser and they couldn't give her a name like steam or vapor, so they chose Misty. And if you think about it, mist is more annoying than hot air, ain't that right, Lynn Mae?" Netta's crazy but in a cool way. She says all the things Mama would say if she weren't trying to set a good example for me. Netta, being outside the mother role for me, can be as real as it gets with me.

"I think she'd be annoying no matter what we call her. And she threw the gris-gris I made for her back in my face like it was a pair of dirty panties," I say, taking the pretty gold bag out of my purse. It's all torn and mangled now, but the sparkly satin fabric is still luminescent of its true intent. "I just wanted to help."

"I know you did, baby. But you can only help yourself, Jayd. Clients have to take the first step by asking for the help they need. It's the initial sacrifice that sets the tone for the blessings to come." I know Mama's right as usual but I can't help feeling a little bit responsible for those around me. Maybe I could've called KJ out more for his trifling behavior.

"But what about people who can't ask for it. Don't we have an obligation to help them?" Netta's eyes meet Mama's as they stare in the mirror at each other and then at me. Netta sighs deeply and Mama takes a breath. I guess I'm more naïve about this priestess thing than I think.

"No," Mama says plain and simple. Netta raises her eyebrows at me and smiles slightly, nodding her head in agreement with Mama. "You have to have faith in your path, Jayd, and that doesn't include trying to fix the world around you." She reaches for the charm bag I made and I delicately pass it to her. I remember as a child Mama used to make me little charm bags for my dolls to sleep in. I guess I've always been fascinated with Mama's work. I just never knew how serious it was.

"Misty thinks my gris-gris caused her gonorrhea." Saying it aloud sounds even stupider than Misty thinking of it in the first place.

"Gonorrhea," they say simultaneously. Mama looks down at the unlucky charm bag and shakes her head. She tucks it between her breasts—like she does her money and other important stuff—and closes her eyes. I hope she's praying because I could use some of Mama's influence with the Creator right now.

"Oh Lord Lynn Mae, that girl's gone completely mad. Her grandmother dying and her mama going to Esmeralda has made her lose her mind." Netta throws a clean drape over Mama's chest before leading her to the washbowl.

"Exactly. That's why I want to make up for it."

Mama looks at me before submerging her head in the warm water Netta's gently spraying over her hair. I know she knows what I'm thinking about doing and disapproves.

"Jayd, you can waste as much time as you want making things for that girl but it's not your problem. It's not going to work if you don't walk in the faith of what you made. That's like someone making a protection charm to keep them out of harm's way and then standing in front of a train. It's not magic, I keep telling you that. It's plain common sense. You need protection from what you can't control, like other people. You also need wisdom to help protect yourself from yourself, catch my drift?"

"Why are you always worried about that girl anyway?" Netta says, scrubbing the effervescent lather through Mama's scalp. Coming from the shelter, she was late for her appointment today. Since Mama doesn't drive she's dependent upon others for rides because she also refuses to take the bus. If she can't walk to where she needs to go or hitch a ride, she says it's not meant for her to be there.

"I'm not worried about her per se," I say, defending my stance. "It's just that no girl should have to go through this type of fire by herself. It's awful what they're saying about her." Mama looks up at me in disbelief, almost allowing shampoo to drip down her face and into her eyes before Netta forces her head back into the sink.

"Jayd, how many times do you have to get burned because of that girl before you'll see she means you no good? Even I can't help you if you constantly choose to put yourself directly in the line of fire," Mama practically shouts at me. "It's her fire, Jayd. Let her go through it alone."

"But she kept the gris-gris. Doesn't that mean she still wants my help?"

Netta looks at me from the bowl and rolls her eyes at me. If I did that to her or Mama I'd be seeing stars, and I don't mean Beyoncé and Jay-Z.

"Or it could mean she's setting you up, Jayd. Open your eyes and listen, girl," Mama says with her head still bent back in the sink. "Enemies are real and they don't wake up one morning, decide you were actually trying to help them, and want to return the favor by trusting you."

"And it could mean that she's afraid to throw it away because she knows how powerful you really are, no matter what she believes," Netta adds. She sounds like she's speaking from experience. "Just leave her alone and concentrate on making sweet charms for you and your loved ones."

"Speaking of charms, how's Rah's tea working?" Mama asks. Damn, how'd she find out about that? I know she reads my spirit notebook sometimes to check on my progress but I wasn't specific about my creation this time. She lifts her head slightly and grins at my shocked look.

"Girl, now you know I measure every single thing in my spirit room. Did you really think you could be in there and I wouldn't know about it? Just because I don't tell you everything I know doesn't mean you've gotten away with anything, little girl." Mama sits up fully as Netta combs the strawberry-scented conditioner through her head. The sweet aroma puts me in a better mood.

"And that goes for me in this shop too," Netta adds, waving the comb around the bright place. "I know where everything is and how much of it is there. It's your job to keep up with it now." Netta directs me to open the large closet taking up one wall of the quaint shop. I open the sliding door to find a personalized Netta's Never Nappy Beauty Shop apron for me.

"Oh Netta, thank you," I say, running over to give her a hug. "I'll be the best helper you've ever had."

"You'll be the only helper I've ever had. And I know you'll do a good job. You just have to stay clear of all this mess, girl. And we're going to help you do just that." I'm glad someone is because I'm not doing a very good job all by myself.

After meeting with Netta and Mama I decide to walk home early to get a head start on my homework. Because it's a short week my teachers have piled on extra work and I don't want to be stuck doing it all over the holiday. When I turn onto Gunlock, I notice a black Monte Carlo parked across the street from our house. As I get closer I see personalized plates revealing it's Mickey's man. What the hell is he doing at my house and how did he find out where I live? First Trish and now this fool. Are my addresses listed in the yellow pages or something?

"Can I help you?" I say walking up to his car. Mama always told me not to have any fear, especially not at home. And this punk doesn't scare me just for the sake of it.

"Yes, or so I've heard." He steps out of the driver's seat and walks around to rest on his hood. I don't like the sound of this. "Rumor has it you can read the future and shit."

"Is this rumor's name Misty?" I ask, unmoved from my spot in front of him. I glance at my house and see no one outside but I feel like someone's watching me.

"That's not the point. I want to hire you to tell me if Mickey's cheating on me and if she's pregnant." He looks down at me, smiling a sinister grin while taking a cigarette from behind his ear and lighting it. I hope he chokes on the smoke.

"That's the stupidest shit I've heard all day and it's been an extra long day. I don't have time for this." I have to get in the house and warn Mickey that her man's on to her and that Misty's involved me in it. Misty knew he wouldn't take her word for it so she directed him my way. That girl's just asking for my wrath.

"You're right. So why don't you just tell me what I want to know. I know you two talk." He's standing so close to me I can smell the beer on his breath along with his stank smokes. He looks down at me like I'm an oversize steak he wants to devour. I'm about to make him a vegetarian though, because this sistah can't be eaten alive.

"Why don't you ask Nellie? They're closer than we are." I walk across the street and toward the front porch, trying to get away from him as quickly as I can. When I reach the first step, Esmeralda's door opens and Misty's mom steps out and gives me an evil glare before picking up a watering can and going back inside the strange house. I knew I was being watched. Am I going to have to see them next door on a regular basis from now on?

"Because Nellie's not as cute as you are," he says, following me. "And I know you know better than to say no to me, don't you Jayd?" He licks his lips at me and attempts to take another step forward but I give him a look so intense that it stops him in his path.

"Go back to your side of the tracks. This is my hood and I can't be threatened over here," I say to Mickey's man. He's really got his nerve stepping in my yard. If Mama were here he'd be in some serious pain by now.

"You don't even know my name, do you, little witch girl?" he says. I see he's heard about my new nickname. "That's because it's so powerful I'd have to cut your tongue if you spoke it aloud." This brotha is too full of himself. I've read about certain Orisha and Ancestors whose names are sacred in that way, but I doubt that his is one of them.

"Go home before you find out how I got my nickname," I say. Like Misty, he needs more than the normal threat to make him disappear.

"Think about what I said. I'll be back for my reading. You might even like doing it with me." What the hell? Now how am I supposed to treat that fool like air? I wish I were like a breeze that would just blow away from this dramatic state of affairs I've found myself in. It doesn't matter if I'm at school, my mom's house, or here at home: drama seems to follow me no matter where I end up.

~ 11 ~
Great Expectations

*"But my mother always said you can forgive and forget/
And expect that most promises won't be kept."*

—JURASSIC 5

Mama didn't get home until late last night and went straight to bed. I didn't tell her about my surprise visit from Mickey's man yesterday and don't plan to. She has enough to worry about. Working at the shelter makes Mama feel like she has another purpose outside of the house and her work as a priestess. Sometimes I suspect Mama just wants to blend in like everyone else and I know just how she feels.

No matter what school I go to or what job I have, I'm always separate from the crowd and not by anything of my own doing. Well, at least not consciously. When I was at Caldwell Elementary up the street I was bullied until I spit on one of the girl's feet and chanted a verse like I'd seen Mama do to Esmeralda one day when she didn't know I was looking. Needless to say my last year there was the most powerful of all but still filled with drama. Then at Family Christian I couldn't get down with their philosophies even though I mastered their teachings and learned about my own ancestors' powerful spiritual lineage from Mama at the same time.

Now here I am all the way in South Bay and I can't escape dealing with the madness that's ever present at this school too. Nellie told me a few minutes ago at break that she's going to tell Nigel about Mickey's baby-daddy doubts the first chance she gets. And Misty has decided to let everyone know just the kind of witch I really am, causing her bad luck and all. It's only third period and I'm ready to get my long weekend started. Jeremy isn't at school today and neither is half the student population. I guess Thanksgiving starts early for people truly giving thanks for the day. For me, it's just another long-ass day of school.

"Hello, Jayd. How are you doing today?" Mr. Adewale asks. Seeing him as Mrs. Peterson's substitute is all I needed to make this day turn around for the better. Thank God for small pleasures in life.

"Good morning, Mr. A. Oh, I mean Mr. Adewale." He smiles at my pretend slip-up and doesn't seem offended at all. Maybe he'll let me call him Mr. A after all. "So when will you have your own class?" I sit down in the seat closest to the teacher's desk. Only five of the twenty students are present so far and with the bell ringing as we speak I doubt there will be more coming. I'm sure he won't make us sit in our assigned seats, today being the last day before the holiday.

"Hopefully sooner rather than later," he says, tapping his pen on the roll book and eyeing the sparse classroom. "A brotha's gotta eat."

"I feel that, except I'm coming from a sistah's point of view." I blush as he smiles at my attempt to have small talk with a teacher. I know Ms. Toni would be pissed if she could see me now. But she's been so busy lately I haven't had a chance to catch up with her and I'm only having fun. I know better than to take him seriously and I can feel the same recognition from him.

"I'm sure," he says, passing around the roll sheet for everyone to mark a "P" by his or her name. "It's pretty much a free day as long as you keep it low. Mrs. Peterson has left your assignment on the board, which is to work independently on your papers due in a couple of weeks. I'm up here if you have any questions." The other four students nod their heads in acknowledgment and prepare to doze off for the rest of the period, leaving Mr. A and me alone to get better acquainted.

"So what do you think of my paper topic?" I say, pulling my government notebook out of my backpack and placing it on the desk in front of him. He opens it and takes out the assignment I'm working on. "The rough draft is due Monday. I'm sure she's going to rip it apart. Maybe you could point me in the right direction for more resources."

"Queen Califia. I remember battling about her in college with my professors. 'Fact or Fiction' was the title of my research paper." He thumbs through the three-page document and I'm grateful for the consideration. I could watch him read all day.

"What was your final grade?" The other students have all but fallen asleep in the quiet room. I doubt any of them had a choice in coming to school today. Otherwise why would any of us be here?

"An A," he says as if it was the norm. He does look hella smart, if there's such a look. I've been fooled many times by dudes posing to be intelligent with the mindset of an idiot. KJ is the latest example.

"You say it like you always got As," I tease. But he looks at me as serious as a heart attack.

"I did." Well damn, I guess he's not playing around when it comes to his GPA. "I'm sure you know how hard it is attending a school like this one. Imagine a university. A brotha like me doesn't have a fighting chance in that type of environment so I always have to be on my A game—literally."

"Now that's admirable. Can I have your paper?" I tease again. He laughs, showing off his perfectly straight teeth. His long dreadlocks are pulled back in a ponytail, showcasing his strongly defined jawbones. Damn this man is beautiful.

"No, but you can look it up online. The bibliography's also listed. Knock yourself out." He pulls his wallet out of his back slacks pocket and opens it up, handing me a card with his personal email on it. I wonder if he has any pictures of his family in there. There's no ring on his left hand but that doesn't mean there's no wifey and baby at home.

"Are you still a student at UCLA?" I ask, noticing the graduate school email address. He must be hella smart to be a grad student there.

"Yeah, I'm graduating with my Masters this spring. But I'm applying for my doctorate at the University of West Los Angeles in the fall." Wow, I've never met a black man like this before. I didn't even know they existed.

"How are you going to teach full-time and attend grad school?" I know I'm getting all up in his business but I need to know how much time I have left with my man.

"When you set your mind to it, you can do anything you want, isn't that right, Queen Jayd?" I don't like the way he said that. Mr. Adewale smiles at me and winks like we share a secret I know nothing about. He acts like he knows more about me than I've told him. Maybe he's heard the things Misty said about me going around school. Maybe Mrs. Bennett has been telling him her version of the story. Whatever the reason is, I don't like his tone.

"What did you mean saying my name like that?" He stops smiling and looks at me very intently as if he's trying to read my thoughts, but only Mama and my mom have mastered that trick on me. I don't know if he's embarrassed or thinks he's embarrassed me, but either way the joking is over.

"I mean that your name is Jayd and you're a queen in training like all of the young sistahs I meet. Sorry if I offended you." I believe he's sorry, but not for saying my name like that. "Now, back to your paper. If you need help you can email me. And don't wait until the last minute to do your re-

search. Take your time doing it and writing, and no matter
how much the teacher despises you, he or she will have no
choice but to give you an A." I should've talked to him before
I rewrote my English paper. That paper was a rush job for
real.

"Thanks for the advice. I'll let you know what I find out."
And I will do just that. I'm going to look into more than just
the papers Mr. Adewale's written. He's not fooling me one
bit. He's got an agenda and I want to know what it is and if
by chance it has anything to do with me or my legacy. I don't
feel any negative energy coming from him, but he's not
telling me his whole story and I want full disclosure.

After flirting with Mr. Adewale for the rest of the period I
made it through my other classes and AP meeting without
too much happening. The only unfortunate encounter was
Mrs. Bennett, as usual. But she's always unpleasant, holidays
and all.

"Jayd, have you seen Nigel today?" Nellie looks more fran-
tic than usual as she approaches my locker. I've managed to
dodge all of my friends today until now. This can't be a good
sign, especially with her asking for Nigel. She's probably
been looking for him all day and hasn't run into him yet. Little does she know he and Mickey ditched school to go shop-
ping for baby shoes. "I want to tell him about Mickey's man
possibly being the daddy before I leave today and I don't
want to hear any protest."

"Nellie, have you lost your damn mind?" I say, not granting Nellie's wish. I look around the empty hall and shut my
locker door, ready to walk to the bus stop. "Mickey's man
knows something's up and we don't need to be in this mess.
That fool came by my house asking about Mickey's other
man and to flirt with me some more. Just leave it alone, Nellie. It's not our business." I walk toward the office doors with

Nellie hot on my trail. I wonder if Chance is here to give her a ride home since the bus isn't an option for her.

"Are you joking, Jayd? I thought Nigel's supposed to be one of your best friends. If he is then how can you honestly stand there and say you agree with Mickey's behavior." I stop and turn around to face my girl. Deep down I know Nellie thinks she's doing the right thing, even if it is coming from the hater in her.

"No, I don't agree with her actions but Nigel's a big boy and can take care of himself. Besides, Nellie, think about the consequences. Everyone will think you're a hater and no one will trust you again. Is that what you want, to end up like Misty?" I say, pointing to my nemesis as she enters the other end of the vast hall. The final bell rang a few minutes ago and everyone's off to indulge in turkey and pie for the next five days. In a way I wish I could say the same thing. But I'm also happy to take long baths and catch up on some much needed sleep at my mom's apartment.

"You're being overdramatic. I'm going to find Nigel." Before I can tell Nellie that Nigel's not here she races down the hall, leaving me and Misty alone. Before she can say something smart, Laura, Reid, and the rest of the posse enter the hall from the side entrance. Reid claps when he notices Misty walking past them. And Laura must be feeling especially self-righteous this morning because she seems to have something to say to Misty.

"You should really be more careful. You never know what's out there, do you?" Laura says, giving her entourage a good chuckle. After Tania left, Laura became the head heffa in charge. Misty begins to cry as she makes her way down the remainder of the hallway. I can't let her go out like that.

"Laura, don't you have a Bitches-R-Us conference to plan or something?" I say, walking up to Misty, who looks like she could use a friend. I can't be all that to her, but I can take some of the heat off her for now. I've decided to take Mama's advice and spend my time working for myself and my friend's benefit. And even if we're not friends, I don't have to allow her to get kicked when she's down. But instead of being grateful, Misty takes a step toward the enemy and away from me. When will I learn not to feel sorry for this girl?

"Now, now, Jayd. You've really got to get that temper of yours checked." Mrs. Bennett comes in from the side entrance. How long has she been out there? "You wouldn't want to have another outburst like this on your record. We might have to investigate other accusations, even ones made by students." Mrs. Bennett's up to something and I want to know what it is so I can be prepared. She's been riding me harder than usual lately and I know it's about more than the breakup with Jeremy. "Have a nice holiday." She exits the hall through the front door with Laura, Reid, and the rest of their crew not far behind her. Misty walks away as if I didn't just save her ass from being tortured. Between that and Nellie, I'm whipped. I wish I had time to take a nap before Rah comes for me later but I don't and I want to get to my mom's as quickly as possible.

"Jayd, I don't know why you keep defending her stupid ass. She deserves whatever she's got coming to her," Maggie says as sassy as ever, coming out of the girl's bathroom. She can't weigh over one hundred pounds and stands exactly my height in the various high heels she wears on a daily basis. "Especially after she offended El Santos. That's a serious no-no, chica."

"The Santos, que es?" I only understand a minimal amount of Spanish, thanks to Mr. Donald, the worst Spanish teacher ever. But Maggie always helps me with my slang.

"Si mami. El Santos or the Saints. I think you call them Orishas, no?" How does she know about our religion? I never heard anyone here talk about it before, or anywhere else for that matter.

"Si, the Orishas. How did you know that's what I believe in?"

Maggie smiles at me and looks from side to side like she's about to reveal a top secret to me. "When we heard about Misty calling you out for the little bag you put by her door, we knew. Chica, mi abuelita y mi mami believe in the Santos. We're Catholic on the outside and Santeria on the inside," she says, showing me the gold cross and picture of the Virgin Mary hanging from her blinging gold chain. "No wonder we've always clicked, si?"

"Fo' sho' sis," I say, returning Maggie's embrace before she leaves the empty hall.

"Have a good weekend, Jayd. And stay as far away from Misty as you can. Her bad luck is really contagious, mami, or so I've heard." Maggie winks at me, leaving me to think about all that's just happened.

It's interesting that of all the people I may be most like, it's a girl no one would ever expect me to hang out with. That may have to change, and soon, if my girls keep going at each other like they have been lately. Maggie's right about me staying away from Misty. My days trying to help that girl are officially over. From now on, she is nothing but air to me.

"See you in three hours," Rah says through his text. I guess I should get to the bus stop to start my long journey home. By the time I make it to Compton, I'll only have about an hour before Rah will be there to pick me up. I can't wait to get to the solitude of my mom's to enjoy my long weekend in peace, with Rah's company, of course. We haven't talked about it yet but I know his mom strips every day of the week, holidays included, and his grandparents are Muslim, so they could care less about American holidays. I hope he's got something really sweet planned for our chill time together.

I've been waiting on Rah for almost two hours and am as vexed as I can get. I'm also worried because I've been calling and texting with no response. Just when I'm ready to call out the cavalry, I see Rah's Acura turn the corner. He speeds down the block, pulls in front of the house, and rushes out of the car. Well, at least I know he's sorry.

"What took you so long?" I say to Rah through the front window as he sprints up the driveway. He said he would pick me up at six and it's a little before eight now. He's always on time.

"Sorry, baby. I got caught up," he says as I close the front door behind me with my bags in hand. I'm packed and ready to get out of here for the weekend. If nothing else, I'm thankful for the extra days at my mom's house and away from this madness. I waited for Rah in the dining room, to the amusement of my uncles. They teased me saying he wouldn't show, but I knew Rah wouldn't let me down this time.

"Caught up with whom?" I ask, giving him my bags while I follow him down the porch steps. I took the extra time to study my lines at first, and then my spirit notebook. I'm going to dedicate Friday to working on my government paper and researching Mr. Adewale's background while studying my spirit work, unless Rah has something better planned for us.

"Trish," he says, putting my bags in the backseat. I open the passenger door and sit down, ready for the entire story.

"And . . ." I say as Rah takes his seat and starts the car. I don't like the feeling I'm getting from his chosen silence. After he reaches the corner he speaks and it's the last thing I want to hear.

"Her brother's having a big Thanksgiving dinner at M & M's

and I have to be there. I'm sorry, baby," he says, bursting my bubble. Damn, why does this always happen with us?

"Rah, I can't believe what I'm hearing," I say. I want to cry I'm so pissed but I'm not letting him see my tears. I don't think it would do much good anyway. If Trish's brother is hosting the dinner it's probably more business than pleasure and I know Rah doesn't have much of a choice in the matter. "We can't spend any of the day together?"

"Well, before that we're going to meet Sandy at her parents' house so I can finally see my daughter." I know seeing his little girl is the most important thing to him right now and that Sandy is using their baby to bait him. And, knowing Trish, she insisted that she go too, if for no other reason but to show Sandy that even a good ass-whipping won't keep her away from Rah. I see Trish isn't going anywhere anytime soon.

"We? Who the hell is we?" I ask, already knowing the answer to my question.

"Jayd, it's not what you think. It's a timing thing, girl, I swear." As usual I'm last on Rah's agenda and I have no one to blame for being hurt but myself. I should know better by now than to think I'd be included in Rah's family plans, even if he did drink my tea. Like Mama said, I have to have faith in what I'm making and so does my client. In this case, I don't think Rah's ready to let go of his other women, no matter what he wants me to believe.

"It never is with you, Rah," I say, this time causing the silence between us. I have nothing left to say. Sometimes having expectations is the biggest letdown of all, especially if the other person never appreciated how great the expectation was.

After the silent ride to Inglewood, Rah reluctantly left me at my mom's front door without coming in. He thought we could spend the rest of the evening together and Friday, but I told him I already have plans. When I get inside, my mom's in full pack mode, ready to spend her holiday with her man. At least her wish came true.

"Jayd, I'm sorry you have to spend the holiday alone. Honestly I didn't think you'd mind," my mom says as she tosses both practical and sexy underwear into her suitcase. "I'll be back on Sunday, sweetie. I can't turn down Tahoe."

"Mom, you can't leave me here for the entire weekend while you go off with Karl." I knew she'd be gone for the holiday but not the entire weekend. "It's supposed to be family time and we are family," I say, plopping across her unmade queen-size bed and dropping my bags on the floor. If Mama saw her bed like this she'd have a hissy fit.

"Oh Jayd, you've got many friends to hang out with. As a matter of fact, what's up with Rah? You can't have dinner at his house?" My mom moves on to the closet, where she begins to sort through clothes and shoes, matching her outfits for her trip.

"Don't ask," I say, rolling onto my back to make myself more comfortable. "Can I sleep in your bed while you're gone?" The last thing I want to talk about with my mother is my boy troubles. She never seems to have any trouble in that department.

"As long as you're alone when you do," she says, throwing a cream cashmere sweater at me. She has the best taste in clothes. No wonder she's always broke.

"Is this for me?" I sit up straight on the plush bed and hold the soft pullover against my chest. Not that I have anywhere to wear it but I still wouldn't mind owning it.

"I think it'll look good on you. And the way to attract what you want is to be dressed for it when it comes. I have a feeling your weekend will turn around and I want you to be ready when it does," she says, heading for the bathroom to pack her toiletries. "There are a pair of white pumps that go nicely with the sweater, just in case." From the looks of it, the only place this sweater is going to get worn is in front of the mirror. Now that I know I'm going to be completely alone for the stupid holiday, I feel lonely and tired.

"Here's the number for the lodge where we'll be staying, Jayd. But you know how to really reach me if you need me," she says, pointing to her head and winking at me. She kisses me on the cheek as she zips up her overstuffed suitcase, grabs her purse, and heads out the bedroom door, leaving me to mope in peace. A good nap will take my mind off Rah, Misty, and Nellie's crazy ass for a while.

I wake up from my nap and it's very late, but I'm not sure how late. I feel like I've been sleeping for days. I walk into the living room and check my phone on the coffee table for the time. I wonder if my mom left me any food.

"Nah, nah, nah, nah. Wait 'till I get my money right." My cell phone rings as I pick it up, freaking me out. I didn't even get to check the time before the name pops up across the screen.

"Hey Jeremy," I say groggily into the phone. I'm so hungry I could eat the damned thing itself. "What's up with you?" I didn't expect to hear from him. I thought he'd be enjoying a long ski trip or whatever it is rich white folks do during the holidays.

"I'm sorry. Did I wake you?" he says sounding as compassionate as ever. "I thought you'd be up late since we don't have school tomorrow." I try to get my sleep no matter if we have school or not.

"Nah, you didn't. Actually I just woke up from a nap. What time is it anyway?" I walk into the kitchen where the flashing stove clock reads twelve and has for just about as long as I can remember.

"It's almost midnight," Jeremy says. Damn, I've been asleep for three hours. Now I'm going to be up all night. At least this time my mom left groceries in the fridge. I don't think they were for me as much as she wasn't sure where she would be spending turkey day, so she stocked up just in case. Her and Mama hate to shop at the markets during the holidays, but not the malls. They can sniff a great sale out like a professional hound.

"I know you probably have plans, but my family's having a dinner tomorrow night. Would you be interested in coming?" Jeremy asks like it's our first date. I remember the last family dinner I attended at his home when he got off for selling weed at school. His family is crazy and on top of that, they drink too much. I'd rather be at my mom's alone than chilling with his wicked mother and racist daddy any day.

"You're right, I've got plans but thanks for the offer." I didn't have to lie but I don't want to hurt his feelings.

"Is there any way I can change your mind? I'd really like to see you outside of school for a change. I think we need to work on this whole being friends thing," he says, making me chuckle. I look in the fridge and spot some yogurt and it's my favorite—lemon. This will hit the spot until I'm ready to cook.

"And does the whole friends thing include being tortured against my will?" I take a clean spoon from the dish rack and sit down at the dining room table. I wonder what the neighbors are doing for turkey day.

"It's not torture and besides, Chance and Nellie will be there. You should come. I promise, it'll be fun. You won't have to deal with my parents at all. You're probably envisioning something small like the dinner we had, but it's not like that. It's more like the party we had last time." Actually it might not be such a bad idea to be there with Nellie. It'll give me a chance to talk her crazy ass out of talking to Nigel. I just hope it turns out better than our encounter at the last house party Jeremy's family had. I know things are different now but his house holds no good memories for me.

"Jeremy, it sounds fun, really. But I've already got plans. I appreciate the thought." I swirl the yellow custard in its container and wonder what's on the menu at his house.

"You'd really rather spend the day alone than kicking it with your friend, free food, and very little adult supervision?"

"How'd you know I would be alone?" I ask but I already know Nellie ratted me out even if she didn't know I'd planned on spending time with Rah. She was probably unconscious of the catastrophic slip but now I have to go just to tell her off in person. I'm not even going to tell her I'll be there. I'd rather surprise her and her big mouth. I hope she doesn't let Mickey's dark secret slip as easily as she did my holiday dinner status.

"Does it matter? As your friend I can't let you eat alone." Well he's got Rah beat there. Rah thinks I'm so strong that I don't need him to make sacrifices for our relationship and he's wrong. I'm tired of being set to the side like leftovers.

"Alright friend, what time can I expect you?" It looks like I'll get to wear my mom's cashmere sweater after all.

"I'll see you at six. And Jayd, I'm really looking forward to spending some time with you."

"Me too, friend," I say before hanging up and finishing my appetizer. If nothing else, I'll get to take some food home. If it's going to be anything like their spreads in the past, their should be plenty to spare.

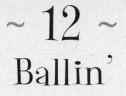

~ 12 ~
Ballin'

*"Cash rules everything around you/
C.R.E.A.M. get the money, dollar dollar bills y'all."*

—WU-TANG CLAN

After waking from my long nap yesterday evening I didn't get back to sleep until six this morning. Luckily there was a black comedy marathon on cable featuring Katt Williams, Chris Rock, and Dave Chappelle that kept me laughing until I finally dozed off. I hope I keep my sense of humor this evening when I'm at Jeremy's house. I'm going to need to laugh if I'm going to ignore the crazy comments his parents throw out.

"Excuse me, is you saying something? Uh uh, you can't tell me nothing," Kanye announces. It's a text from Rah. He's already trying to lock in plans for the weekend but I'm not responding to him right now. It's after three and I still have to do my hair and decide on my final outfit. I think my mom's white cashmere sweater and Kenneth Cole pumps will be perfect, but I'm not sure about which skirt to wear. Do I go sassy and short or classy and long?

"Sassy and short. You have great legs," my mom says, invading my private thoughts and I'm glad. I could use her help. Dressing to impress is my mom's specialty, not mine. As cold as it's going to be by the beach tonight, I'd sooner wear a pair of jeans and a hoodie. But my mom would never let her little girl go out like that.

I was thinking the same thing, I say in my mind, throwing down the long skirt while holding the thigh-high chocolate suede mini to my body and eyeing my outfit in the mirror. Jeremy won't be able to take his eyes off me all night. Good, it'll show him what he missed out on, acting a fool.

"There are some cream tights in my top drawer. Wear those and you've got the perfect outfit. I'm glad you have somewhere to show it off," she says, indirectly saying 'I told you so' and that she was right. I slept with the sweater next to me. When I woke up, my hand was still on it so the first thing I felt was the soft material, and then Jeremy called. My mom's got the whole power of the mind thing down pat. Too bad she didn't continue her lessons with Mama. Who knows how powerful she would have become.

"Mom," I say out loud. Even if she can hear my thoughts, I still like talking to her as if she were sitting in front of me. "Should I even be going to this dinner at Jeremy's house? Isn't it wrong to string him along if I'm really feeling Rah?"

"Jayd, are you getting married to either one of them tomorrow?" my mom says. *"I already know the answer is no because if it were any different, Mama would have both of us in a sling and I don't look cute in hospital attire,"* she says, making me laugh. I can see it now if I ran off and got married like Tania and my mom did. Mama would kill us both, damn the consequences. *"Have fun girl. Eat some turkey, have some pie, and don't worry about anything else. Now, I've got to wake up my man before we miss our reservation. Have fun and be good."*

"Bye mom. Thanks for checking in," I say, but she's already gone back to her vacation in Tahoe. My mom's right. I am going to have fun without worrying about the rest. It's not every day I get to celebrate Thanksgiving at an estate in Palos Verdes, basically Beverly Hills by the beach. And I get to look good while doing it. So far I'm not seeing a negative side to this new way of thinking. I want to be ready when Jeremy gets here and I don't have much time left to prep. I hope Rah enjoys his evening as much as I anticipate enjoying mine.

Putting the last bump in my freshly pressed hair, I check myself in the mirror and smile at my reflection. I opted for a simple, sleek hairstyle to complement my attire and I admit it all goes together very well. With my mom's natural-colored throw to block out the cold, my outfit is complete. Now all I need is a good perfume to seal the deal. It's six on the dot so Jeremy should be here any minute. I think I'll go with J'adore, one of my favorite scents to borrow. I sometimes wear it just so I can spray the pretty bottle. My mom loves to look at all her fancy fragrances lined up like the expensive statues they are. As I spray the delicate scent over my body I hear a knock at the door. Jeremy's on time and I'm ready for our night out.

"Wow Jayd, you look beautiful," Jeremy says as I open the front door. I turn on the living room lamp before heading out. I don't like walking into a dark room at night.

"You don't look so bad yourself." And he doesn't, dressed in khaki slacks and a button-down white dress shirt. His attire must be at his mother's request because Jeremy looks anything but comfortable in his clothes. "Something from the back of your closet," I tease as I lock the door behind us.

"Yeah, only on holidays or at court appearances," he says jokingly. But I hope we never have to experience the latter again. "You ready for the festivities? The house was already packed and only about half of the guests had arrived when I left," he says escorting me down the stairs to his Mustang parked in the driveway.

"As ready as I'll ever be," I say, sliding into the leather seats that coordinate well with my top. It's a crisp, clear evening and I'm looking forward to the scenic drive. The view of the ocean will be breathtaking against the fading sun, setting a mellow mood for our eventful evening. "I'm glad you called and invited me to dinner. I've missed hanging out with you."

Jeremy looks at me the same way he did before our first kiss. I hope he doesn't make the same move on me tonight because I might give in to his soft lips.

"I'm glad you answered and grateful you decided to come. I've missed being with you too." I don't know where tonight is taking us but I'm down for the ride.

When we arrive at Jeremy's house, the first thing I notice is the glowing pumpkins lining the walkway up the porch steps to the house. The huge wooden door has a large hand-made wreath hanging around the antique brass hook. The usual luxury cars are in the driveway, along with several others, giving the look of an episode of *MTV Cribs*. I wonder who else was invited? I can hear people in the back of the house having a ball. If tradition holds, that's where we'll be hanging out as well. I liked it better when the two of us hung out alone in his room and not just because we also got in a good make out session up there. The scenery is nice but the social life at the Weiner household is highly overrated.

"After you," Jeremy says, pushing the heavy door open. The smell of yams, turkey, mashed potatoes, green beans, and rolls hits me in the face is I step into the foyer. "Let me take that for you." Jeremy removes my wrap and hangs it in the hall closet with the other coats. Servants walk quickly back and forth between the kitchen and the great dining room with huge platters in their hands, completely unmoved by our entrance.

"Son," Jeremy's father, Gary, says walking down the winding staircase. He's holding a pipe between his teeth, with a glass of scotch—his signature drink—in his free hand. I'm glad he's holding onto the rail with his other hand because he looks as lit as a Christmas tree. "And you brought Jayd. It's nice to see you two are still hanging out." Yeah, he doesn't mind us hanging out as long as we don't bring any brown babies home. He's such a two-faced liar I can't even stand to look at him. But Jeremy's right. I need to judge him and not him by way of his parents. I'm asking for the same thing in return, so I'm not going to be a hypocrite.

"Hello, Mr. Weiner," I say. Jeremy smiles at my effort. I hope he knows how hard it is for me to bite my tongue. But friends have to do that sometimes for the sake of the friendship. I hope Nellie understands that principle when I share it with her.

"How do you like what my wife did with the place? By the time Christmas and New Year's rolls around she will have spent a fortune on turning this place into a goddamned holiday parade, and I'm Jewish," he slurs, waving his drink in the air. The house does look stunning. I've never seen anything like it. There must be a half dozen waiters tending to every aspect of the food and layout. And the decorations look like something I've see on display at Pottery Barn. The food smells good and knowing Jeremy's mom, it's a slamming southern spread. Good food is good food, I don't care who makes it.

"It's very nice," I say, elbowing Jeremy to get us out of small talk with his dad and outside to where the food is. I don't want to hear another speech about how he married a Southern Belle who can't make brisket.

"Dad, I'm hungry and so is Jayd. We'll talk later." Jeremy leads me through the packed living room and out the sliding back doors. His brothers and their women are seated at the table closest to the doors. There are about fifteen or so small round tables spread through the large space, each with an outdoor heater in the center to ensure everyone's warmth. The waterfall pond at the very back of the yard is lit with orange lights in the spirit of the season. Every table has a huge pilgrim basket overflowing with fruit and expensive chocolates. They've really outdone themselves. Even Mama would have to give them props.

"Jayd, how are you, girl?" Justin, his older brother, says. I admit it's nice to see him again. He's good for the eyes, much like Mr. Adewale is.

"I love your shoes, Jayd," his girlfriend Tammy says. She's always complimenting my attire and I like her vibe too. They look extremely mellow and they have the munchies for real. They've raided the dessert tray and are making their way through the pound and chocolate cake, pumpkin pie, and cookies as a team.

"Thank you. And I'm still loving that necklace," I say, referring to the iridescent puka shells gleaming against her honeyed complexion. Tammy and Justin are the picture-perfect surfer couple.

"Hi, Jayd. It's nice to see you again," his eldest brother, Michael, says to me. As usual, he and his wife Christi are tense and drinking heavily but at least they are coating their stomachs with plenty of food. The only person who's missing is their mom. I wonder where the queen of the bunch is.

"Jayd, I didn't know you were coming," Julie Weiner says right on cue. She walks up to Jeremy and kisses him on the cheek before greeting the rest of her family. With her she brings a surprise guest of her own: Mrs. Bennett. They both smile at my obvious discomfort before joining everyone else at the table. "Your family doesn't celebrate Thanksgiving?" Mrs. Weiner gives me the creeps. It's no surprise she and Mrs. Bennett are friends.

"Actually my family is celebrating in their own way and I'm here at the persistence of your son. Your house looks lovely," I say looking past them both and toward the pond. I've already designated that as our official hangout spot for the night. There are several buffet tables set up throughout the open space so I should be able to hide out well for the rest of the evening and sample all the tasty food.

"Why thank you, Jayd. Do help yourself. We have more than enough to share." Mrs. Weiner looks around her estate and beams with pride. I know she gets a kick out of making her neighbors envious: it's written all over her face.

"I am surprised you would come, Jayd, especially after all that's happened," Mrs. Bennett says, ready to gossip with Jeremy's mom about me. What a trick. Doesn't she have anyone her own age to talk shit about?

"Oh, I hope there's no trouble for you at school, Jayd," Mrs. Weiner says, trying to feign shock and concern. I'm sure Mrs. Bennett's already caught her up on everything she can about me. Like any other hater she just wants the scoop to make herself feel better about hating on me. I look at Jeremy who's searching for an exit without being too impolite. He better hurry up and think of one before I say something. I can only exercise so much tact with these two broads to deal with at the same time.

"Mrs. B, I don't mean to be rude but I've got to greet my friends. You don't mind mom, do you?" Jeremy says, not really asking as much as telling her. He takes my hand and escorts me to where Chance and Nellie are seated, directly across from the pond. Mickey and Nigel are having dinner at his house. I wonder how that's going.

"What's up, man?" Chance says, rising to greet Jeremy and then bending down to hug me before we sit. I haven't talked to Nellie since yesterday and don't know if she's changed her mind about telling Nigel but I've got her cornered tonight. I know Mickey was nasty to her the other day but she knows the girl better than I do. When Mickey gets her mind set on something there's no turning back for her. She tends to lash out in the process but that's just how she is. We all have our faults.

"Jayd, I've never seen you dressed like that before," Nellie says. From the look on her face, I'm not sure if it's a compliment or an insult.

"Yeah, you look all sophisticated Miss Jackson," Chance says playfully, but Nellie looks as serious as a heart attack. She can't hate on me and Mickey at the same time. I can't wait to call her out on her hypocritical behavior.

"Why thank you. I would say the same about you but I see you didn't dress up for the occasion." Chance has on a pair of worn Enyce sweats and a hoodie to match. He looks cute like always but nothing out of the ordinary. Nellie on the other hand has gone all out for the occasion, wearing a full-length red dress with a purse and Dolce & Gabbana stilettos to match. She even got some pieces added to her hair to complete the princess look.

"You look nice Nellie." I decide to make nice first since it's going to take all the sweetness I've got to get through to my girl. "New shoes?" she looks down at the shiny heels and smiles. Cute shoes can do that to a girl.

"Yes. I saw them on the Third Street Promenade and couldn't resist," she says, smiling at Chance.

"I don't care how much it costs to keep that smile on your face," Chance says kissing her nose like she's a baby. What the hell? Please tell me this fool didn't just shell out at least four bills for her feet. He's ballin' but not rolling in dough like Jeremy's family is. Those shoes probably set him back quite a bit and Nellie's not even as into him as he is into her. Maybe he knows that and is hoping he can buy her love like Jeremy wanted to buy my forgiveness, but that never works.

"Isn't he the sweetest thing?" Nellie says, caressing Chance's hand and smiling at me like a jealous girlfriend. She needs to be put in check, and now.

"The sweetest," I say, turning toward Jeremy and smiling big. "Jeremy, would you mind getting me a plate? These shoes are killing me." I'm telling the truth about my mom's taste in shoes. We wear the same size but her foot is narrow and mine is wide. I'm surprised she let me wear them at all but a good man will make you forget the small annoying things in life.

"Sure thing, Lady J. You guys want something?" Jeremy says, picking up our plates before heading for the buffet. I look at Chance and he gets the signal that I want to be alone with Nellie. He probably thinks we want to talk more about our shoes but I could care less about her feet. It's her mouth I'm concerned with.

"I'll get our plates, Nellie, if you're ready to eat," Chance says. Nellie looks at the empty china and rubs her stomach. The girl could use to gain some more weight even if she did put the weight back on she'd lost for Homecoming. Mickey used to be the smallest of us but that didn't last for long. I've always been in between.

"Thank you, sweetie. But no carbs for me please." Nellie takes a sip of her iced tea and watches the guys walk over to the table where the food is piled high. I look at Nellie and we stare at each other for a while. Why do we have to have heat between us?

"Nellie, what's up with you?" I say, breaking the ice. She looks down at her shoes to avoid my eyes. "You're hating on me and Mickey for no reason and it needs to stop now."

"No reason," Nellie says with more anger in her voice than I expected. "You both take me for a joke, like I can't possibly have a man of my own." What the hell? What is this girl smoking?

"What the hell are you talking about, Nellie? Who said you couldn't have your own man?" Nellie rubs her hands across her lap as if to straighten her dress but I know she's trying to avoid looking at me because she knows I'm right.

"You did when you didn't introduce me to Nigel properly, and Mickey flaunts it every time she takes the attention away from guys we meet. She already has a man. Why does she have to take the available ones too?" I see my girl's been holding back on some issues she's had for a while. I'm not the mind reader in the family and I need to make that clear to her.

"Nellie, how is anyone supposed to know what you're feeling if you don't tell someone? I had no idea you felt this way, for real. You know you're flyy, girl. You can have any man you want." Nellie finally looks up at me and forces a thin smile across her face.

"You sure you don't swing both ways? You sound like you like me a little too much," she says, lightening up. "But for real though, Jayd, this whole thing with Nigel is too much. Mickey can't get away with this."

"Nellie, she's not getting away with anything. Nigel's not a fool. He knows what he's getting into even if he doesn't know Mickey's full intentions." My reasoning looks like it's starting to seep into Nellie's thick skull. I hope it does for her sake because having Mickey as her enemy is never fun.

"I know he's a big boy, Jayd, but this still isn't fair." Our eyes meet again and I can see the pain she's feeling. But taking it out on her best friend isn't the answer and it's not going to make her dreams come true. If anything, Mickey will unleash a nightmare Nellie won't soon forget.

"Nellie, you sound like a two-year-old who didn't get everything she wanted for Christmas. Life isn't fair but it's not about you or Nigel or even Mickey for that matter. It's about the baby, and they as the parents will choose how to deal with the situation." Speaking of children, Jeremy, Chance, Mike, and Gary walk back to our table with our plates and a basketball in Gary's hands. Please tell me these fools aren't about to ball, especially not the drunk ones.

"But that's just it, Jayd. If there's a chance Nigel might not be the daddy he deserves to know. I feel like as his friend I should tell him the truth. I'm surprised you don't feel the same way." Oh no, she didn't go there with me.

"Maybe that's because I've known him longer. You've known Nigel for all of what, two months, and you're ready to swear your loyalty to him and not your girl you've known for two years. That sounds suspicious to me, Nellie." I hate to call her out like that but that's what real friends do. They don't rat you out to other people the first chance they get.

"So what are you saying, that I was waiting for the opportunity to turn Nigel against Mickey and get him all to myself?" I prop my head to one side and let her answer her own stupid question.

"Well, if the stiletto fits," I say as the dudes approach the table. I hope she thinks very carefully about the conversation we just had. If she wants to be so honest she should start by being true to herself about why she does what she does, especially when it concerns her girls.

"Hey ladies. Would you mind moving dinner to the basketball court by the garage? We want to get a quick game in," Chance says, pulling out Nellie's chair with his free hand. He passes her the near-empty plate while she puts her shawl around her shoulders. Nellie is a pretty girl, just way too high-maintenance for most of the brothas I know.

"What is it, sobers against lushes?" I say, making everyone laugh. I'm glad they think it's so funny because I was being serious. This is going to be the most ridiculous game of ball ever. I could see brothas in the hood getting their game on at a holiday function, like my uncles at Christmas. But they play first and drink later. We're always serious about basketball.

"This Jayd's a keeper Jeremy. She's a witty little one, isn't she?" his dad says as he walks up to my chair and hugs me tightly. From the smell of his breath, if I had a match I could light his entire mouth on fire. I reluctantly allow the second or maybe third white person ever to hug me up.

"Yes, she is." Jeremy smiles down at me while he holds my plate over my head, laughing at the scene. He's such a tease. Nellie looks from me to Jeremy and smiles big like something's up between the two of us again. I have to make sure she understands I just came with him tonight as a friendly gesture, nothing more.

"Alright, to the court. I want my five hundred dollars before the old man chickens out," Michael says, snatching the ball away from their dad and leading the way back across the yard. The other guests are enjoying their evening engaged in good conversation and food. We've only been here a little while but it's a cool vibe. Aside from his mom, Mrs. Bennett, and Nellie's hater rays, I'm enjoying my evening. But I look away from Jeremy's mesmerizing blues to see two of the most obnoxious people walk through the back gate—it seems I've spoken too soon.

"There's my beautiful wife now," Reid says, holding his girlfriend's hand and heading our way. Laura looks pissed to see me here and I feel the same way. I know she's tired of seeing me daily in rehearsals, but not as tired as I am of her boyfriend calling me his wife.

"What are Reid and Laura doing here? Don't tell me Tania's home for the holidays too," I say as I follow Jeremy and the rest of the crew toward the garage.

"It's a neighborhood thing. I sure as hell didn't invite him," Jeremy says, looking down at me. He puts his free arm around

my shoulder but I want the other one that's holding my
plate. I've waited long enough to get my grub on.

"Happy cluck-cluck day," Reid says to Nellie. He looks tipsy
and Nellie looks highly amused. I'm glad she's in a good
mood. I need her pleasant if she's going to hold up her end
of the bargain and make nice with Mickey even if she hasn't
fully agreed to it yet. By the time we all get together on Saturday for the practice game at Venice Beach and the session
later on that night at Rah's house, I'm sure she'll be completely convinced to see things my way.

"Reid, where's your father? We were supposed to shoot a
game of pool. That cheapskate owes me his best bottle of
whiskey from the last game he lost," Mr. Weiner says. I see
the stakes are high when playing at the Weiner household.
The last thing he needs is more liquor at his disposal.

"Are we going to play or what?" Michael says, shooting a
perfect jump shot to get the energy flowing. I see ballin' runs
through their veins in more ways than one. Justin joins the
game and Tammy sits down at the table across from Nellie
and me to cheer our boys on.

"I just hope they don't try and kill each other like they did
last time," Tammy says, hugging herself tightly. It's chilly out
here and all she has on is a hoodie, some shorts, and a pair of
worn Uggs, so I know this heat lamp isn't doing her much
good. I on the other hand am burning up in this sweater. But
that's not going to keep me from enjoying my food and
watching the game. It's not as exciting as my brothas playing,
but it's entertaining nonetheless.

"Hey, ease up, man," Chance says to Michael, who's supposed to be on his team. He wants to block his father's shot
so badly he'll do anything to get to him, including run over
his own teammate. There's some serious competition between the two of them. Before Chance can free himself from
the mess, Michael pushes him out of the way to block Gary's

layup, sending Chance to the ground, where he lands on his right knee.

"Foul," Justin's high-ass voice emotes. There are no referees at home even when we do need them. Chance curls up in pain, holding his right knee to his chest. This doesn't look good, especially not for the big game on Sunday. KJ will talk shit forever if Rah, Nigel, and Chance are forced to forfeit because of an injury.

"Are you okay, Chance?" Nellie says, running up to him. I would but I've got gravy all over my hands and I'm not a nurse. Besides, Chance has taken a lot more than a fall before. He'll shake it off in a couple of minutes.

"Yeah I'm good. I just need some rest. Don't tell Rah and Nigel, okay? I can still play in the game on Sunday."

"You better, or Nigel and Rah will have your ass in a sling for real," I say, taking another bite of the succulent turkey and gravy. This food is banging and was worth dealing with all the obstacles to get to it.

"Don't worry. Your secret's safe with me," Nellie says as she escorts Chance to our table to sit out the rest of the game. Jeremy joins us and lets the other two go at each other since that was the plan in the first place. I hope Nellie's still good at keeping secrets when it counts because if she's not, we will all have a lot to lose when it comes down to what's really important: whipping KJ's ass.

~ 13 ~
Who's Got Next?

"Run for your life."

—JARVIS CHURCH

"So did you have fun?" Jeremy says on our ride home. "I hope my family wasn't too much for you like they usually are." I was hesitant at first about hanging out at Jeremy's house again but I'm glad I went. His mom and Mrs. Bennett disappeared, leaving me alone for the rest of the night. I almost forgot they were there, which made the evening much better.

"They are a bit much but it was fun to see your brother win the game." I laugh at the memory of Michael collecting five one hundred dollar bills from their dad. For a couple of drunks they put on a very entertaining game. Chance and Jeremy enjoyed stuffing their faces with Tammy and me while talking shit about the game at the same time. Nellie picked at her vegetables and pampered Chance's knee for the remainder of the evening and he enjoyed the extra attention. I think we all had a pretty good time.

"Yeah, they can get like that when there's a crowd around. Sorry you had to witness that." Jeremy turns the heat up to high as we slowly make our way down the winding path leading away from Palos Verdes and back to Pacific Coast Highway. The stars are shining brightly and the moon is full, making the ocean water seem silver from our vantage point. The waves crash against the shore, making me long for the simplicity at the beginning of our relationship when night beach visits were the regular.

"Do you ever wish we could go back to our first date?" Jeremy says, almost taking the words right out of my mind.

"Yes I do." It's too bad that in reality his dad's not as cool as he was tonight. And his baby mama's drama is just as bad as Rah's in my opinion. "If things were only that simple." If I knew a spell that could get us back to that moment in time and keep us suspended there, I would cast it in a minute.

"There are no cupcakes you could make to go back in time, huh?" Jeremy says, making light of his newfound knowledge of my spiritual heritage. On top of him being the father of Tania's baby, I don't think I could ever truly share my total self with him and that's the major problem. Rah understands me for who I am, even though I'm starting to see that his habit of taking me for granted isn't going away anytime soon. Maybe there's something I can make for that, but that's not going to help me deal with Jeremy.

"No, I wish there were though. But time is one thing we can't get back." Jeremy takes his right hand off the steering wheel and places it on my left hand resting on my lap. I know I probably shouldn't let it stay there but I don't want him to move. Besides, I'm sure Rah's holding Trish's something right now since he seems to be rejecting the tea I gave him. And like my mom said, I don't have any rings on my finger and I'm still feeling Jeremy.

"I'm going to win you back Jayd. I miss being with you too much not to keep trying." Why do dudes always want you when they can't have you? Well, I'm going to enjoy the attention Jeremy chasing me will undoubtedly bring and maybe it'll make Rah see that I won't wait around forever for him to get his act together. I hope Rah also checks his ego at the door when it comes to the game on Sunday because I don't think Chance will be able to play from the looks of his limp tonight.

"Jeremy, we've already been down this road. Can't we just enjoy where we are right now without the pressure?" Jeremy turns the corner and goes around the bend, following the road to a cliff overlooking the ocean. He stops the car and turns the already soft music even lower, giving me his undivided attention.

"Jayd, I've never felt this strongly about any other girl I've ever met. I don't mean to pressure you but I want you back and I don't want to wait." He takes my hand and lifts it to his lips, kissing my knuckles gently and making me tingle all over. Damn, this isn't good. He opens my palm and kisses that too before lifting my hand to his face, pulling me forward into our second first kiss.

I stay in the moment of his soft lips for a while, enjoying fantasizing about us being together again. But I'm going to stick to my mom's advice and not commit to being anyone's girl right now. Honestly, I don't think either Jeremy or Rah are ready to be in a serious relationship and neither am I. But I do think I've made my final decision about the situation.

"What are you thinking about?" Jeremy says, pulling back to take a breath. The moonlight hits his eyes and compliments his olive complexion. He takes his right hand and caresses my chin. He's so sweet when it's just the two of us.

"I was just thinking we shouldn't have to give up what we have if we're not ready to." I know he thinks we're on the exact same page but I'm not thinking we should get back together completely.

"Cool, then this means you'll be my girl again?" he flicks the gold "J" bangle he gave me and smiles at me before kissing me again. I don't want to end our session but I need to set him straight now.

"Jeremy, I like this but we can't get back together," I say between kisses. I know he heard me because as close as we are we could share ears. "Jeremy, did you hear me?" I try to back up from him but he's relentless in his passion.

"Jayd, let's talk later. You're letting me kiss you and that's really all I want to think about right now." He looks down at me and smiles, looking like he's going to eat me up. Then he bends down to kiss my neck. He knows I'm speechless at this point. He's right; we don't have to talk right now. I just want to enjoy Jeremy in this moment as much as he's enjoying me.

After Jeremy dropped me off on Thursday night, which was actually more like early Friday morning, I went to sleep and didn't wake up until late Friday afternoon and decided to chill at home for the rest of the day. Cedric came up and gave me some business, letting me touch up his braids. Rah texted me again but I didn't respond and don't plan on it. He knows I'll see him later on today at the practice game and Jeremy will be there too. I talked to him briefly yesterday and look forward to seeing them both today. This should be fun if nothing else. I just hope my girls are able to be civilized today. I'd hate to see them get into it at the beach. It's a nice warm day outside and the folks will be out at Venice. I don't want them making a scene and the cops out there don't play.

"So how was your Thanksgiving? Was the family happy to meet you?" I ask Mickey as she and I settle into the bleachers while Nigel and Rah warm up. Nellie and Chance aren't here yet but Rah already reserved their spot on the court. The brothas playing now look like they just got out of the pen and are taking the ball to the basket like it talked about their mamas.

"Girl, they were cool as hell. I guess they weren't feeling

Tasha too much and were happy to see Nigel has another
girlfriend now."

"So I'm assuming you didn't tell them they were going to
be grandparents in a few months," I say. Nigel and Rah are
shooting the ball back and forth, waiting for the brothas to
finish their game. Usually when it's packed like this the brothas
play until twenty, no matter if it's one-on-one or a team playing.

"Of course not. We want them to get to know me and the
holidays are perfect for that. We were thinking of dropping
the news on New Year's." She opens a big bag of Cheetos and
starts munching on them. I reach for a handful and she looks
at me like I'm a lion reaching for her infant. I quickly grab a
few and she protectively tucks the rest of the snacks under
her jacket. This girl is nuts.

"Good, everyone will be too hung over to pay y'all crazy
asses too much attention." Mickey smacks me in the arm,
making me laugh. I don't know how she plans on hiding her
growing belly. She's always eaten for two but now there's
clear evidence of her impending motherhood.

"How was your holiday? Did Rah take you out to eat or did
y'all stay in?" Mickey's not going to be happy to hear that I
spent my holiday with Jeremy but I'm not going to lie about
me being his friend, to her or anyone else that asks.

"Rah ended up spending the day with Trish and her
brother."

"Oh Jayd, that sucks. I'm sorry, girl. You should've called
me. I would've come to get you and you could have chilled
with us."

"That's sweet, Mickey but I had a good time without Rah.
I went over Jeremy's house and had a ball." Mickey stops
chewing in mid-crunch.

"Have you lost your mind, Jayd? Don't you remember what

he just did to you?" she says resuming her munching. "And Rah's not going to be too happy about this."

"Well, he'll have to get used to it because I'm not going to stop seeing either one of them. And not only that, Chance hurt himself playing around at Jeremy's on Thursday and Jeremy may have to fill in for him."

"What," Mickey says almost choking. "Does Rah know about all of this?"

"No. We didn't speak much in the car on the way here. I wanted to wait to see what happened today. Maybe Chance isn't as hurt as he looked and then I can wait to tell him after the game. I don't want that on his mind while he's playing against KJ. As far as he knows, I'm still pissed about him ditching me for Trish."

"Aren't you? I mean that must be why you would date a fool whose daddy is a racist," Mickey says.

"I try not to judge my friends by the mistakes of their parents or even the stupid ones they make themselves," I say, gritting my teeth and Mickey knows exactly who I'm referring to. "None of us are unworthy of a little mercy, are we, Mickey?"

"Whatever, Jayd. I just hope you know how much you're hurting Rah with this and he doesn't even know yet." Mickey's right. Rah's going to be hotter than hell when he finds out but he has no one to blame but himself for me getting close to Jeremy again. I just hope he doesn't let it ruin our friendship. Mickey and I notice Nellie and Jeremy walking up to the court with a limping Chance a few steps behind them. Rah and Nigel follow our eyes and look at each other like they're doomed.

"What the hell happened to you?" Nigel says to Chance. He nods "what's up" to Jeremy and Nellie. Mickey and I walk down the bleachers to greet our friends.

"Oh, I thought Jayd would have told you," Chance says,

hugging me and greeting Mickey. "I twisted my knee messing around on Thursday." Rah's jaw tightens as he looks from Chance to Jeremy and gets why Jeremy's here.

"Hell no," Rah says, gripping the basketball tightly in his hands. "If you can't play I've got someone else in mind." Nigel looks at Rah and swats the ball out of his hands, catching the rebound. Rah looks at his friend and waits for his response.

"Hey man, this is our game not yours, and Jeremy can ball." Rah looks at Jeremy and then at me. I can feel him probing me with his eyes to see if something else is going on. I hope he can't read my feelings because I'm happy to see Jeremy here. I think the three of them make a formidable team against KJ and his boys. But if they allow their personal feelings to get in the way we're all going to lose and that's not an option.

"Man, please. I know you're not serious about letting this punk ball with us. How's that going to look?" Rah looks Jeremy up and down like he wants to punch him and Jeremy holds his ground, unmoved by Rah's sheer hatred of him.

"Who's got next," yells a sistah in a bikini with a whistle hanging around her neck. It's a nice day for November but it isn't that hot. I have on a bikini top underneath my shirt and a sweater around my hips just in case the weather changes, which isn't unusual for southern California, but I also have on my Nike sweats, not bikini bottoms like this girl. She's got to be a little chilly, no matter how cute she thinks she is.

"We do," Nigel says, throwing the ball at Jeremy, who jogs to the scrimmage line and throws the ball back to Nigel. Rah looks at the two of them and doesn't budge from his spot. Seeing Rah's untouched by his words, Nigel smiles and throws the ball to his boy. Rah catches the pass and dribbles the ball, taking it to the hoop over Jeremy's head. The crowd breaks out in laughter as Rah prepares to take Jeremy to school. If Jeremy plays anything like he did against KJ the first time, Rah's in for a surprise.

"Damn, Jayd, Jeremy's about to get played, huh?" Mickey says licking orange powder off her fingers. She's ignoring Nellie completely and Nellie is apparently returning the favor. As long as they don't create any more drama I could care less if they talk to each other. It may be better this way for the time being.

"Don't you remember the game against KJ a couple of weeks ago, Mickey? Jeremy can ball." Nigel catches the rebound and passes it to Jeremy, who dribbles the ball while focusing on the basket.

"Yeah, for a white boy. You know Rah can wipe the court with his ass." Mickey blows a kiss to Nigel, who pretends to catch it. The two of them are starting to make me sick so I know they must be getting to Nellie. Jeremy proves my point to Mickey by shooting a perfect three-point shot from where he's standing, at least three feet back from the actual line.

"I think they've both got game," I say and I mean in more ways than one. And honestly it would be nice to see both of them kick KJ's ass together.

"Whatever, Jayd. That was a lucky shot. When they start hustling on the court, let's see if your white boy can hold his own." She does have a point but I think Jeremy can get down and dirty if he has to. Rah and Nigel play so rough, sometimes lips and eyes get busted. That's how the brothas who just left the court were playing. They're on the sidelines now trying to calm down, but one dude is teasing the other for losing and the heat is rising.

"I've got an idea. I'm going to sit this one out and if Jeremy beats you he's on the team. If you win you can bring your boy," Nigel says. Now this should be very interesting. Rah looks at Nigel and laughs in disbelief. Jeremy looks anything but amused.

"What's up, man? Are we ballin' or what?" Jeremy runs up

to Nigel, waiting for the ball. Rah shakes his head from side to side and follows suit, ready for the challenge.

"Whatever, man. It's your funeral," Rah says as Nigel passes Jeremy the ball and Jeremy passes to Rah. Nigel joins us in the bleachers, ready to see his boys go at it.

"You see this hustle, baby? It was learned in the streets. Them Redondo Beach boys can't handle real ballin'," Rah says, shooting the ball over Jeremy's head and making the first basket. Jeremy catches the rebound and slams the ball into the basket for two points of his own. Rah's smile slowly fades as he realizes Jeremy really does have skills. Now the real game is on. This is what I'm talking about.

"I hope Jeremy wins so we can kick KJ's ass tomorrow. He and his boys will be no match for the three of us."

"Now don't go getting too cocky," I say, pushing Nigel on the shoulder causing him and Mickey, who's sitting in between his legs, to tilt to the left. They both look at me like they want to smack me, but they know better.

"What are you talking about? If your white boy has as much game as you think he does, then KJ, C Money, and Del will be no match against the three of them." Mickey looks up at her boo and they kiss, causing Nellie to roll her eyes and hold Chance's hand tighter.

"You're forgetting that KJ and his boys are from Compton like the rest of us. I know it's hard to see but he got his game from the streets just like y'all did and can hustle with the best of them." I hate to sound like a fan but I don't want Nigel to underestimate KJ for a second. It seems like everything he's lacking in good character he makes up for on the court, and then some.

"Damn, Jayd, if I didn't know better I'd say you were KJ's newest cheerleader. First you choose the white boy over Rah, now KJ over us all. Whose side are you really on?" Mickey says, outing me to the rest of the crew, except for Rah.

"What do you mean? Jayd chose Rah over Jeremy a while back," Nigel says, not totally up to date.

"Well it seems the tides have changed since she and Jeremy spent the holiday together, ain't that right, Jayd?"

"But we were there and y'all didn't seem back together to me," Chance says, smiling at me. He would love to rub it in my face if Jeremy and I got back together. Nellie looks shocked too but doesn't respond.

"So that's why you didn't say anything about Chance's knee when you had the opportunity," Nigel says, putting it all together. I glare at Mickey, who rolls her eyes in return. She knows she didn't have to call me out like this but I'm not ashamed of anything. Rah and Jeremy are making each other work on the court. Why can't I use some of that competitive energy to my advantage?

"Nigel, I'm a big girl. Don't worry about why I do what I do," I say, shocking everyone.

"I don't even know who you are anymore," Nigel says as he puts his arm around my shoulders. "Girl, you are too much sometimes, you know that?" Nigel knows I have a right to be happy and that Rah's situations aren't going to go away easily. As my friend he wants me to be happy in the end just like what I want for him. We watch our boys hustling on the court. The entire crowd is into the game: that's when you know the players are good. The guys who lost the last game are still on the sidelines arguing with the opposing team. Their yelling is getting louder and distracting Rah and Jeremy on the court.

"Gun," the sistah in the bikini yells. She blows her whistle and the crowd frantically rushes from the bleachers. Both Rah and Jeremy run over to where we are as we make our way through the panicked crowd. Just then five shots are fired and the crowd's running turns into a stampede. I hate getting caught up in shit like this.

"Jayd," Rah screams, pulling my arm and rushing me off toward the parking lot with our friends right behind us. Jeremy helps Chance limp to safety with Nellie on his other arm. Mickey and Nigel are already at his car.

"Why niggas always got to be shooting?" Nigel says as we make it to safety. Since the shooting wasn't random we know we're not in any real trouble but decide to get out of Dodge anyway. No need tempting fate, as Mama would say.

"Because y'all are always getting into beef over your stupid egos," I say, looking from Rah to Jeremy and back at Nigel. "So are y'all ballin' tomorrow or what?" Nigel looks at his boys and waits for one of them to make the first move.

"It was a tie," Rah says. We all know that but I think Rah thinks he would've won had they been able to keep playing. "I think we should see if my boy's available."

"What boy, Rah?" I say to him. I hope he's not talking about Trish's brother but I think that's the only other dude Rah balls with.

"What difference does it make? He can ball and that's all that counts. See y'all at school tomorrow. We should get some rest tonight." Rah walks away from Nigel's car and toward his own. "Are you coming?" he says to me. I look at Jeremy, who now realizes that Rah and I are more than simply old friends. He smiles at me and I know he understands what's up. I need to make it clear to both of them right now.

"So, you can play with Trish's brother and rub my face in the fact that you're still dating her but you can't play with my ex-boyfriend? That's real mature, Rah." Rah turns around and looks back at me.

"Do we have to have this discussion right now?" I look at Jeremy and back to Rah. I know he wants me to trust him on this one but I can't. And I'm tired of him expecting me to go along with the fact that he has two other chicks in his life that he can't let go of for one reason or another.

"Yes we do because I'm tired of your ego getting in the way. We all want to win, Rah; it's not just about you." Rah looks defeated and tired. He turns around and walks to his car. I guess he's not ready to hear what I have to say yet. I just hope he comes around by tomorrow because I want more than anything for them to come together and serve a serious blow to my other ex's ego. I don't care how the job gets done, I just want the satisfaction of winning to be in my favor for once.

~ 14 ~
One On One

*"Uno es el numero magico/
En vida y en muerte."*

—JILL SCOTT

After yesterday's game at the beach, Rah hasn't talked to me or attempted to call me. I guess he's still sore about Jeremy playing. I hope he gets over it by the time we get to Westingle. Nigel and Mickey picked me up from my mom's house to bring me to the game and will take me back to Mama's after she picks up her car from Nigel's house later this evening.

"So what did Rah say about the game?" I ask Nigel as he turns onto Manchester Boulevard headed toward the beach. It's a nice day to play ball. Not too cold or hot.

"He said he'd be there. He didn't say much else in his text. But Jayd, for real though. I know Rah's hurt you, but what do you see in Jeremy?"

"Me seeing Jeremy has more to do with me than with Rah. He's a good guy and he likes me. Why shouldn't I like him back?" And that I do. Jeremy and I talked on the phone for a little while last night and I assured him I wasn't backing down from more kisses in the near future. "I can't explain why I'm attracted to him any more than y'all can explain why you like each other." He and Mickey look at each other and kiss before the light turns green. It sucks being in the back of the car with two lovebirds. I still haven't told Mickey about her man's pop-up at my house because she's been glued to Nigel the entire holiday, or so it seems.

"Well, that's easy. We love each other. You and Jeremy aren't anything like us," Nigel says. This boy is really sprung. For his sake I hope he is the baby's daddy because I don't think he would take losing Mickey to her man very well.

"Jeremy loves me," I say, shocking them both. I don't know if he loves me like Nigel loves Mickey, but I do believe he loves me like only he can.

"Yeah, but you don't love him and I know that for a fact and so does Rah." Nigel's right. I wish I could say that I felt the same way about Jeremy as I do about Rah but I'm not in denial about that nor am I looking for that kind of love right now. I have too much on my plate to worry about being in a relationship. I want to focus my energy on becoming the best apprentice I can to Netta and on getting my license. Everything else is secondary at this point.

"Well, I'm not looking for all that right now. I just want to chill and enjoy the game. Can a sistah do that?" As Nigel pulls into the high school parking lot, I notice Mr. Adewale talking with Jeremy. What's he doing here?

"Cool, he could make it," Nigel says under his breath. I don't care how he got here. I'm always happy to see Mr. A.

"You invited a teacher to the game? Why?" Mickey says, unbuckling her seatbelt and opening the door. She pushes her seat forward to let me out of the classic Impala.

"To be the referee. I have a feeling we're going to need one today. Besides, we had to have an adult supervise the game since it's on school property. He offered last time so when I saw him Wednesday morning I asked him and he said he'd be here if he could. Good thing too because we would've had to move the game to the park down the street and it's always packed there."

"What's up man?" Jeremy says walking over to our car to

greet Nigel. "KJ and his crew are already inside." From the cars parked in the lot, it looks like all of South Central showed up for the game, as well as some other fans. Rah's not here yet but I'm sure he'll make his appearance soon.

"Hey man. Glad I could make it," Mr. Adewale says, giving Nigel dap before winking at me. This game is going to be great, granted if KJ loses. Seeing Mr. A is the icing on the cake for me. "Are we ready to play?"

"We're just waiting on my friend but he's on his way," Nigel replies as he looks out toward the street.

"Well, let's get inside and y'all can warm up before the game. I want to scope the place out before we start anyway," Mr. A says. Jeremy looks at me like he wants to kiss me right now. Noticing the vibe, Mr. A gives me a confused look and walks away toward the gymnasium.

"Y'all coming?" Mickey says as she and Nigel follow Mr. Adewale. She looks at me like a disapproving mother watching her daughter go on her first date with the neighborhood thug. I guess that's how her mother felt when Mickey first started seeing her man.

"Actually Jayd, can I talk to you alone for a minute?" Jeremy asks. Our friends look at us and continue their trek.

"We'll be right there," I say to Mickey, who's being anything but patient with me. I know she means well but she should be worried about Nellie, not me.

"Jayd, I saw these at the beach before I left yesterday and had to get them for you. I hope you don't think I'm trying to buy you back or anything like that." All ready to protest his bad habit of giving expensive gifts for the wrong reason, Jeremy pulls out a dainty puka shell necklace, much like the one his brother's girlfriend always wears.

"Oh Jeremy. That's so sweet," I say as he steps closer to me and fastens the sea jewelry around my neck. I can't be mad at him for this.

"You seemed to really like Tammy's so I thought you should have your own." Jeremy bends down and kisses me on the lips, making me forget we are at a game where I'm expecting Rah, who pulls up just at that moment. Seeing me and Jeremy kissing in the lot, Rah's eyes glare through his driver's side window and I know we're in for it now.

"Let's get inside," I say, leading Jeremy into the gymnasium where the opposing team and crowd are waiting to get this game started. To my surprise, Trish and Tasha are already inside. What are they doing here? I guess they feel it's at their school and they have a right to be here, even if they're not welcome. Rah walks into the gymnasium just as I join my girls in the bleachers. He stares at me hard and I know he's pissed but what can I say? It looks like we both have our other interests at the game.

"Alright, here's the game," Mr. Adewale says, calling both teams to the scrimmage line. KJ and his boys step up to Nigel, Rah, and Jeremy, ready for battle. "The first team to make it to twenty wins the game. There's no pushing, pulling, kissing, or hugging, got that?" Mr. A says, making the boys unwillingly crack a smile. I wonder if he's going to be coaching while teaching at South Bay High. "Let's get started," Mr. A says. And with the blow of his whistle, he throws the ball up in the air and the game is on.

After KJ caught the tip-off, he and his boys dominate the first half of the game, barely giving our team a chance to possess the ball, let alone make a shot. I feel partially responsible. I should never have let Jeremy kiss me when I knew there could be a chance that Rah might see us like he did. Rah's been off his game all morning and we're going to lose if he keeps it up. I have to help us out and fast.

I decide to concentrate on seeing Rah play like I know he can. I envision him swooping all over KJ like the air that he is to me. I envision Rah grabbing the ball from C Money and taking it to the hoop right over their heads. Feeling my gaze, Rah looks at me and I see the hurt in his eyes. I look back at him sorrowfully and mouth the words "I'm sorry" to him. I hope he understands. He mouths back "I love you girl" and I smile in recognition of the love. Seeing my reaction, Rah snaps back into the game with more light under his fire. That's the Rah I want to see playing in this game.

Stealing the ball from KJ, Rah runs up court, passing the ball to Nigel, who passes it back to Rah. KJ tries to guard Rah but it's no use. Before we know it, Rah does a three-sixty dunk on KJ's head, pissing KJ and his boys way the hell off. Rah's in rare form now and I'm feeding him all the positive energy I can, even with Trish and Tasha sending daggers of hate in my direction. I again focus all my attention on Rah. We are only six points behind and can catch up quickly as long as we're holding the ball.

I focus on Rah passing the ball to Jeremy for three. That will help us out a lot. Not exactly as I planned, Rah passes the ball to Jeremy, who's tripped up by C Money, and the re- bound goes to Del. Not missing a beat, Jeremy steals the ball before they have a chance to head back down the court, shooting a perfect three-pointer.

"Hell yeah," Mickey yells as the rest of the gymnasium goes wild. "Take them fools back to preschool." Mickey loves a good game of street ball just like the rest of us. KJ looks at me like I'm the one punking his ass on the court. Maybe it's time for me to change my focus.

KJ catches my gaze and can't look away. I'm doing just like my mother told me to: I'm concentrating on the final out- come I want and not letting go until it happens. The game is going on around KJ, who shakes his head thinking that's going to set him straight, but not a chance. I focus intently on the shape of his peanut head and concentrate on its curves. The intricate hair design in his freshly cut head mimic a labyrinth, guiding me along the crooked path to my final destination where my boys win the game.

"Jayd, what are you looking at?" Mickey says, following my eyes to the court. "I know the game is good but it ain't that good." No matter what anyone says to me right now I'm not letting go of my visual lock on KJ. He has to get knocked off his game and I'm just the player to do it. The only difference is he doesn't know how to play my game.

"Oh nothing. I'm just watching the game like you. Why aren't you concentrating on helping your man win?" I say to Mickey who's been giving me attitude ever since I got to the gym. I know she sees Tasha over there sweating her and that's who she needs to be sweating back.

"Why aren't you?" I ignore her last comment and concentrate all my thoughts on KJ slipping up. My boys are catching up now but that's not enough for me. KJ's too good for his own good but not invincible. Catching my sight, I notice Rah looking at me staring at KJ. Instead of my target slipping up, Rah does and earns a foul on C Money, who promptly returns the favor.

"Hold the ball, not each other," Mr. A yells as he follows both teams up court. I feel bad for slipping up Rah but I'm not letting go of my lock. KJ's trying everything not to look my way but he'll give in and when he does, the game is ours. Jeremy goes for another three and makes it with little effort while his teammates guard the other team from obstructing his way.

"Alright, it's a tie," Mr. Adewale says as the buzzer rings loudly through the auditorium. "Each team will pick one player and y'all get one shot only. Whoever makes the shot wins the game." Damn, we all know who's going to end up playing one-on-one: KJ and Rah. Rah looks at Nigel and Jeremy, who each nod in agreement. They back up, leaving Rah on the court with Mr. A and KJ, whose boys sat down on the sidelines as soon as the announcement was made. They never challenge KJ's status as the best player on their team.

"Let's go," Mr. A says, spinning the basketball on his index finger and leading the two players to the center of the court. The lower bleachers are filled with spectators, mostly neighborhood kids and us. With enemies like two of my three exes playing against each other, the heat's going to be on to get the ball first from Mr. A. I just hope they don't kill each other in the process.

Mr. Adewale blows the whistle indicating the tip-off and the final scrimmage begins—this is street ball at its best. Pinning the two best players against each other and watching them damn near kill each other to get the ball into the basket is a crowd-pleasing classic. Rah catches the ball and quickly moves up court with KJ hot on his trail. Me and my girls rise to our feet in excitement. I decide to focus all my energy on slipping up KJ. Rah can handle the rest on his own.

Again feeling my gaze on him, KJ looks my way and shoots back an evil stare. He then returns his focus to Rah, who's close to sticking his elbow dead in KJ's eye. KJ backs away from Rah but doesn't go too far. Rah reaches up for a layup but changes his mind and dribbles the ball back down court, making KJ run.

"Is he going to shoot or what?" Nellie says, finally getting into the game. Even haters can't help but get excited when there's a tiebreaker at stake. Granting Nellie's wish, Rah shoots the ball for three and the gym is completely quiet, waiting to see what will happen next. The ball enters the basket, followed by nothing but air and loud roars from the crowd. Even Trish and Tasha are on their feet cheering. It was a good game.

"That's game," Mr. A says, blowing his whistle. Me and my girls rush to the court to hug our boys, with Chance and his crutches close behind. KJ looks vexed as he grabs his towel from Misty, who looks like she's feeling much better. Customarily, the losing team would greet the winning team to show good sportsmanship, but somehow I don't think that's why KJ's headed our way.

"Thou shalt not be a witch. I know it says that somewhere in the Bible and you are going straight to hell," KJ says, causing his boys and Rah's girls to laugh hysterically. Misty and the South Central crew also get a kick out of his impromptu sermon. But I've got a few verses of my own to spew.

"*He's air, Jayd. Take the high road, always. Remember what Mama taught you about being proud of who you are, no matter what. You're a queen, Jayd, plain and simple. No one can take away your crown unless you give it to them.*" My mom's right. These punks aren't worth getting my head hot over anymore. But I can't let him misquote the Bible because that isn't the way I read it.

" 'Even if I bear witness of myself, my witness is true, for I know where I came from and where I am going; but you do not know where I came from and where I am going': The Book of John, Chapter Eight. Look it up," I say, silencing the entire crowd with my revelation. Three years of private Christian school did some good. Nigel and Rah smile as I turn to walk back to my spot at the bleachers, ready to grab my stuff and roll. I know we're going out to eat after that win.

"The devil knows the Bible better than anyone," Misty says, stepping in front of KJ like she's his protector. That would be cool if he were hers right back, but since he's not, it just makes Misty look more like the desperate trick she really is but doesn't have to be. I can't believe I ever felt sorry for her.

"Are you really going to stand there and defend this jackass after he let you take the blame for catching some shit from him? Misty, even you can't be that stupid." Misty's eyes burn with rage as she takes a step toward me like she's going to reach up and slap me across the face. "I wish you would," I say, crossing my arms and bracing myself just in case she does work up the nerve to throw the first blow. KJ and his boys stand behind her but don't attempt to hold her back, which they really should. Before she can do anything, Rah's other ex walks into the gym, ready to cause a scene of her own.

"You still kill chickens in your backyard with your grand-mother and shit or have y'all moved on to bigger and better things?" Sandy steps onto the court like she owns the joint. She's always had a way with guys. I don't know why. She's as big as any of them, just in a miniskirt.

"You ain't fooling nobody Jayd. I know you did something to Rah to make me not stand him but you're not going to get rid of me that easily. I'm going to stick around until whatever you gave him wears off. And then we'll see who has the real power around here." All I need is another friend turned enemy on my case telling what little she knows about my lineage to anyone that will listen. It's time to get out of here for real.

"Yeah, it's not going to work on me either," Trish says standing next to Sandy, with Tasha by her side. War makes even stranger bedfellows than politics. Chance, Rah, and Jeremy stand next to me, ready for whatever goes down next. Mr. Adewale's watching the whole thing go down, ready to jump in if it gets too serious.

"Trish, shut up. You don't know what you're talking about," Rah says, but I'm ready to come clean with everyone about who I really am. "Anything Jayd does she does because I ask her to, not because I'm so stupid I can be tricked." Jeremy looks at me and I know he's wondering what Rah's talking about. I'm glad Rah stands up for my heritage and his role in it.

"Rah I didn't mean it like that. You don't know what you're saying and it's not your fault. Sandy told me what this girl is really like and it explains everything. I knew there was a reason I didn't like you doing his hair," Trish says to me and I'm about to blow her head wide open with my truth. Misty nods in agreement, ready to jump me with her newfound posse backing her move. She thinks she's got me cornered but nobody bullies a Williams woman.

"You know what? You're right about me. I do have powers and I can influence people's lives, so does that make me more or less dangerous?" Surprised by my approach, both Sandy and Trish take a step back to let my words sink in. Everyone but Misty looks surprised at my confession. Misty looks both satisfied and scared, but of what?

"Let's go, Misty," KJ says with the rest of their followers walking away from the scene. Mr. Adewale grabs his bag and heads out, congratulating my boys on his way out the door but I know he wants to grill me more about what I just said.

"Are you okay?" Jeremy says rubbing my shoulder. His touch feels good but I stop him because I don't want to start anything with Rah being right here. It's rude and I wouldn't want Rah to do the same thing to me.

"I'm fine. You played your ass off, Mr. Weiner," I say teasing him. I knew they could win if they put their minds to it.

"I have a feeling you had something to do with our win." Instead of arguing or agreeing I simply let the truth sit for a moment before Rah and Nigel come over to check on us.

"Sorry about all that. Y'all want to grab something to eat? It was a good game, man," Rah says, giving Jeremy his overdue props.

Maybe they can be cool with each other after all but I'm not going to push it. I'll be happy if they simply allow the other to exist in my world without hating on one another. But who am I kidding? I'll have to balance the two of them delicately. But I think I'm up for the challenge.

Epilogue

"You're all up in my head Jayd. No one's ever had me off my game like that before," Rah says on our way back to Compton. We went to Pann's for our victory meal and everyone had a good time. Nellie and Mickey managed to avoid talking to each other the entire time and so did Rah and Jeremy. Why can't Rah be more open-minded and accepting of my friendship with Jeremy? Even now after I've been fronted by not one but two of his ex-girlfriends, he still wants to possess me fully and I can't take that. One is the magic number for me and I've got to honor that.

"I know and I'm sorry about that. I was trying to slip up KJ, not you. But you rose to the occasion anyway," I say patting his shoulder while he cruises down Crenshaw toward the 105 Freeway. We have to pick up Kamal from his grandmother's house before heading back to Mama's. At the last minute, I decided to ride with him instead of Mickey.

"Jayd I'm serious. Let's work on you and me, to hell with everyone else." If it were only that easy. I'm not done with Jeremy and Rah's got so much baggage he could open his own luggage store.

"If you really wanted that to happen, the potion would have worked," I say and Rah is silent. He knows I'm right and

I'm tired of him trying to hustle me into his harem. He didn't want the potion to work and it's not as effective as it could have been. I followed the directions for the tea and I watched him drink all of it. What did I do wrong?

"*You didn't separate yourself from the outcome, Jayd. How many times have I told you you can't be attached to your emotions when trying to honestly help others? That's why I couldn't master my powers.*" My mom always has a way of creeping in at just the right time. *Rah's a human being, Jayd. He makes mistakes. He'll have his weak moments and yes, he will be confused just like you are about Jeremy.*" How did she know about that?

"Jayd, are you okay?" Rah looks at me like I just had a stroke. His phone vibrates and I can see Sandy's name on the screen. Just the thought of them together vexes me but my mom's relentless in her approach.

"*Where else are you going to find a friend who you can be your total self with, powers and all? Don't be so quick to give up on him, Jayd.*" My mom's right. I need to listen to Rah. I know he doesn't intentionally mean to hurt me, but it still burns.

"Do you still love her?" I ask him flat out. He flips the phone open, ignoring her call, and returns it to its spot on the dashboard.

"Who?" he says like he doesn't know who I'm talking about.

"Your baby's mama, that's who." Rah looks serious as he contemplates my question. I curl up in my oversize knit sweater. The cold air has returned, putting an end to our long holiday weekend. Tomorrow it's back to school and the regular grind.

"Sandy's got my seed, Jayd," he says passionately. "You know how I feel about that. And I saw my daughter for the first time in a long time on Thanksgiving. Jayd, she's beautiful and I can't risk Sandy tripping and taking off like that again. I'm going for full custody, Jayd, and I'm going to need you here by my side because it's not going to be pretty. Now, does that answer your question?"

It does and then some. Like Mr. A, I'm going to have to be on my A game to weather the storm headed our way. Between my girls, Rah and Misty's drama, my hustle's going to have to be tighter than ever before. Thank God I've got Mama on my side to help me master this hectic game of life we're constantly playing.

Drama High, Volume 6:
COURTIN' JAYD

L. Divine

ABOUT THIS GUIDE

The following questions are intended to
enhance your group's reading of
DRAMA HIGH: COURTIN' JAYD
by L. Divine

DISCUSSION QUESTIONS

1. Make a list of all of the characters in the Drama High series thus far. How do the names fit their personalities?
2. Do you think KJ handled Mickey's revelation properly? Why or why not?
3. If you could make your own charm, what would it be called? What would it be used for? In what form would you make it (tincture, tea, bag, etc.)? What ingredients would you include?
4. Look at the song lyrics at the top of each chapter. What do they tell you about the chapter's themes and titles?
5. At the end of Chapter Twelve, is Nellie justified in her feelings about how she thinks Jayd and Mickey treat her? Explain why you agree or disagree with Nellie's reaction.
6. If you were Jayd and Rah spent the holiday with Trish and her family, how would you have reacted?
7. In what ways is maintaining a friendship with Jeremy good for Jayd? What would be the benefit of their getting back together? Do you think she should give him another chance?
8. Have you ever worked at a homeless shelter during the holidays like Mama does? If you have, what was the experience like for you? If you haven't, is this something you'd consider doing? What would be your expectations?

9. What's a typical holiday like for your family? How is your culture similar/different from Jayd's family traditions during the Thanksgiving holiday?

10. How do you think Jayd and Netta will work together? Will this time be beneficial for both of them? In what ways?

11. Is Rah right for not wanting Jeremy to play in the game against KJ? Explain your opinion.

12. What do you think of KJ's reaction to Mickey's revelation that he and Misty have an STD? Is it fair the way Misty's being treated?

13. Do you think Jayd should stop trying to help Misty even though she feels sorry for her? Would you continue to try to help someone who's a friend turned enemy?

14. Should Jayd help Rah win custody of his daughter? What would you do if you were faced with the same dilemma?

Stay tuned for the next book
in the DRAMA HIGH series,

HUSTLIN'.

Satisfy your DRAMA HIGH craving
with the following excerpt from
the next exciting installment.

ENJOY!

Prologue

After playing ball all day, I'd think Rah would be exhausted but he's actually hyped from beating KJ and his boys in overtime. I enjoyed watching my boys stomp KJ's ego. If I'm not mistaken, I think I saw KJ shed a tear he was so pissed. I can't wait to see the look on his face at school tomorrow because me and my girls are letting everyone know KJ got his ass whipped. I know KJ thinks I had something to do with him losing and for once he's right. But if Misty still thinks it's my fault she and KJ have the clap, she's crazier than I ever gave her credit for.

I'm exhausted if for no other reason than I had to deal with Rah's two crazy broads and Misty's hating ass all weekend long. It's one thing to have my school enemies at school and my home enemies at home, but when they come together, the outcome can only be negative for me. I'm going to need to give myself a cleansing after the long weekend we just had. My drama repellent also needs some tinkering and I hope Mama's up for the task. I can handle Rah's current leech Trish, and Misty always, but his baby mama being up in the picture is more than I can bear alone.

Sandy remembers a little about how my grandmother and I get down but she and I weren't friends long enough for her to get too close to me, unlike Misty. I befriended Sandy on her first day at my old school, Family Christian. Even though she's a year ahead of Rah and me in school and two years ahead of us in age, she jumped Rah the first chance she got and made me her enemy soon after. I didn't know as much about my gifts as I do now and I'll be damned if Sandy's going to wreak havoc in my life again like she did two years ago.

Rah and I haven't spoken a word since he told me about his plan to sue Sandy for sole custody of their little girl because I don't know what else to say. What he doesn't know is that I had a dream about Sandy leaving two years ago but I never told him or Mama about it because honestly I didn't want her to stay. This has been the longest ten minutes of my life and there's so much traffic on Crenshaw from the Sunday night cruising that we're stuck with each other for longer than usual.

On one hand, I'm glad Rah's ready to take full responsibility for his daughter. Sandy did keep her away from him for almost two years without so much as a phone call and she's not the most stable person in the world. But Rah has enough on his plate as it is. He's only a junior and he already takes care of his little brother and holds down the household while his mom strips all day and night. Raising a toddler will be more than he can handle and I'm afraid of him doing whatever he deems necessary to hold it together, including more shit that could land his ass on lockdown with his father.

"What are you thinking about over there?" Rah says, turning down the smooth oldies he's playing. Before I can answer, Rah's phone vibrates again and this time he answers. He better not be talking to either one of his broads in front of me right now because I'm not in a very friendly mood. Rah's really got me worried about his next move and he seems too in control of everything, especially when it comes to Sandy and his baby girl.

"Who's that?" I say softly, not wanting to be too rude but letting him know I won't be ignored. Rah looks at me out the corner of his eye and then back at the bumper-to-bumper traffic facing us. We haven't moved more than three feet in the last five minutes and it doesn't look like it's going to get any better anytime soon. Whoever's on the phone is making him smile, so I know it can't be one of his other girls.

"Yeah Nigel, we're right around the corner from your spot, man. We'll be there in five minutes." Rah hangs up his cell and throws it in my lap before giving me a sarcastic grin. "Here. Now you can monitor all my calls." He smiles at me and puts his blinker on, ready to cross traffic. But because he's not in a classic pimped-out ride, no one takes him seriously.

"Very funny," I say, tossing the phone into his lap. I'm glad he's got jokes because I need a good laugh. Rah and I have been way too serious lately. I'm glad I have him to talk to about both the good and bad in our lives but what happened to my cool, kicking-it companion? Good kissing messes everything up. I should have learned that lesson by now.

"Is it cool if we roll by Nigel's spot? They're having a little session to continue the celebration." After we left Pann's stuffed like a holiday turkey, we went back to my mom's and grabbed my stuff so I could get back to Compton earlier than usual. My mom hasn't made it back from Lake Tahoe yet and I still have much work to do. But kicking it with my friends is always a priority, even if my girls still aren't currently speaking to each other. Maybe a session is just what we need to chill us out.

"You know I've got to get back to Mama's soon," I say looking at the clock on the dashboard. "It's already after five." I usually get home around seven on Sundays and I don't want to give Mama any reason to be irritated with me. If I come home smelling like weed, she'll grill me like I was the one smoking even though she knows me better than that.

"Yeah, I know. And I still have to pick up Kamal from my grandmother's house so we'll just kick it for a minute, cool?" I nod my head in agreement as he turns down Slauson Avenue headed toward Nigel's pad.

I can't help but wonder how my girls are getting along and whether or not Nellie's in a forgiving mood. They ignored each other during the game and at lunch but she kept her mouth shut about Mickey's baby-daddy decision. I hope it stays that way until things cool down a bit because I'd hate to see what would happen if Nellie wanted to give Mickey a taste of her own bitchy medicine. That's a gift no one should have to accept.

~ 1 ~
Misgiving

"Can't you tell, the way they have to mention/
How they helped you out, you're such a hopeless victim."

—LAURYN HILL

When we get to Nigel's house I can see Chance's Nova and Nigel's Impala in the driveway. As nice as their classic cars are, they should've been the ones cruising down Crenshaw this evening. I guess his parents are out for the night, leaving us to chill alone in his beautiful home. Nigel lives in a huge old house that his parents recently had renovated when they relocated from Compton two years ago. His older sister is away at Spelman so it's just him and his parents, and they give Nigel all the freedom he could ever ask for.

When we walk into the foyer, the bright chandelier hanging from the ceiling sparkles, sending rainbow rays from the setting sun across the white walls. We step down the few steps to the main room, which serves as a living room and entertainment area, with a minibar set in the back corner.

"Come on in and make yourselves at home. We're up in my room," Nigel says closing the door behind us as I follow Rah up the stairs. Nigel runs past us up the wide staircase into the grand hallway. The houses on this side of Los Angeles have been here forever and the white folks are moving back in and attempting to buy them up even if they are only a stone's throw away from the hood. As I step up the last step I feel like I'm in an ancient southern mansion, slaves and all.

It must be strange living in a house this big that possesses so many ancestral spirits. I can hear them all over the place.

"Where are the folks?" Rah asks as Nigel swoops past us to open his bedroom door, letting us into his private fortress away from the rest of the house. From the looks of it, the other three rooms on this floor are still in the process of being re-modeled. I know I'm the only one who can hear what others may refer to as ghosts speaking through the dilapidated walls, but it's all good. I'm getting used to the surprises of my powers. I can see why my mother began to reject our gift when she was my age. It can freak a sistah out if she's not open to receiving.

When we walk into Nigel's room, the pungent aroma of incense mixed with tobacco and other smoke hits me in the face and travels up my nose. Damn, now the shit's going to be all in my hair too. I may have to sport my do wet all week if the smell's too much for me to take.

"Oh, they had some sort of fundraiser at the community center off Vernon. You know my dad can't resist getting a pat on the back for writing a check, even if he wouldn't normally be caught dead on that side of the hood." Nigel's dad used to play professional basketball but retired after a knee injury. Now he's a top executive at a sports gear company and his mom is a not-so-happy housewife. With their daughter at an elite black college, they make the perfect black American dream family.

"What's up y'all?" I say through the cloud of smoke in the large room. Nigel's room is off the chain. Even Jeremy would be envious of his sports-themed room that is at least the size of the living room downstairs. Nigel's an obvious Laker's fan, with purple and gold making up the color scheme. Vintage Magic Johnson, James Worthy, and A.C. Green posters hang on the wall. The best part of the room is the wall of mirrors where a basketball hoop also hangs. "Like to watch yourself hoop, I see?"

"Perfection is an art that should be admired," Nigel says, slipping between Mickey's legs in complete comfort.

"For sure, baby," Mickey says, kissing the top of Nigel's blue wave cap. I've noticed the hood coming back out in my boy since he got with my girl. Nigel's pretty boy was starting to get out of control at Westingle. But between the laid-back atmosphere at South Bay High and hanging with Mickey, he's starting to relax a little and his environment says the same thing. There's an aquarium like the one at Rah's house, a king-sized bed in the center of the room, and two futons on opposite walls, now occupied by Nellie and Chance in one and Nigel and Mickey spread out across the other. Rah and I take a seat at the card table opposite the entertainment center, ready for a quick chill.

"That was a good game, man. Thanks for letting my boy play," Chance says in between puffs. If I didn't know better, I'd say Nellie has been smoking, but I'm sure it's just a contact high.

"Yeah, y'all did play well together," I say, looking at both of my girls, who haven't said a word or moved an inch since I walked in. I guess dudes aren't sensitive to the tension between girls but I can cut it with a butter knife it's so thick. What did I miss in the hour we've been apart?

"What's up with you, Jayd?" Nigel says, smiling as he grabs the remote from the side table next to his futon, flipping the television stations while Digable Planets plays in the background. *Blow It Out* is an all-time favorite album of our crew and would be the perfect mellow music if the tension wasn't so hot in this spot.

"Nothing much. Just ready to get back on my grind." I can only relax so much when I know I have mad work waiting on me at home. This is why I must get my own ride and soon. I hate being at the mercy of other folks, even when we are chilling. When I'm ready to roll, I don't want to have to ask anyone. And by the looks of it, we may be here longer than I want to. It's only a matter of time before one of my girls sets the other one off.

"How's your leg?" I ask Chance as he passes the blunt to Nigel. Rah's looking down at his vibrating phone. The way his jawbone just tightened I'd say it was probably Sandy. As long as he doesn't answer it in front of me, we're good. "It was cool but I think I may have made it worse during the stampede at the beach yesterday."

"Yeah, that tends to happen after a shooting," I say as Rah looks at me seriously. I know he worries about me but not as much as I do him.

"You should've seen Nellie's prissy ass trying to get out of the way without messing up her hair. It was hilarious," Mickey says, making us all laugh. But Nellie doesn't find it amusing at all. Here we go. All it takes is one off-the-wall comment to get these two going when there's already beef between them.

"At least I take my health and well-being seriously, unlike you, mommy-to-be. You only care about yourself, just like when you called Misty out in front of everyone at school. That was stupid, Mickey." There was more venom in that comment than in snakebite. The two of them have been hating on each other more and more lately and I'm sick of it. I wish Mickey would just come clean so we could move on from being full-time secret keepers and back to being best friends chilling.

"Taking care of myself means getting out of dangerous situations I may find myself in, and calling bitches out like I see them is part of that process," Mickey says, adjusting Nigel's head in her lap. "It's called street smarts, baby girl. And no, there's no book you can buy to teach them to you. You've got to live it to be it." Nellie looks like she's about to burst with anger. It's been an extra long day and I can't deal with another fight. I'm ready to go now and I think Rah just got my drift.

"Okay ladies, that's enough," Chance says, feeling my pain. "Where's the blunt? Let's get this vibe mellowed out. It's been a good day and you two are bringing me down."

"Y'all can't smoke around Mickey. She's expecting," Nellie says, taking the blunt away from a now very annoyed Chance. I knew Nellie would be Mickey's nightmare of an auntie but I didn't think it would start this soon. Nigel gets up from his comfy spot and walks across the room, snatching the blunt from a stunned Nellie. Nellie gets up to follow him but he's back in Mickey's clutches before she can get to him.

"Nellie, sit down and shut up," Mickey says, taking the blunt from Nigel and licking it, irritating Nellie even more. "Every pregnant chick I know is around weed twenty-four/seven and their babies come out just fine." Mickey hits the blunt and passes it back to her man. Nellie looks like she's going to charge our girl and there's nothing I can do but sit and watch it all go down.

"Are you going to let her do that? She's carrying your baby." Nigel looks across the room at Nellie and exhales the thick smoke. His deep laugh turns into a cough and Mickey laughs at Nellie's concern too. I know Nellie means well but I told her this would happen. If she were really exposing Mickey's foul behavior for our girl's sake, that would be one thing. But Nellie's intentions are purely selfish, which won't benefit anyone, least of all herself.

"Mind your business, Nellie," Mickey says, sitting up in her seat to look more closely at Nellie. The room is dimly lit but it's enough to see the hate radars glaring across the room.

"It is my business, Mickey."

I look from Nellie to Mickey and back again, knowing they want to rip into each other right now. Before I can stop her, Nellie lets the kitten out of the bag, forever changing the scope of our friendships. Damn I hate this mess.

"Mickey's not sure who the baby-daddy is and chose you because you're going to be ballin' one day." So much for Nellie holding her tongue and allowing us a chill ending to our victorious weekend. Nigel doesn't seem surprised by Nellie's revelation, much to the apparent disappointment on Nellie's face. And Chance is completely unaffected by his girl's heart being broken over another dude.

"One day? Baby, I don't know if you've noticed, but I'm ballin' now," Nigel says, shooting a basket against the mirrored wall. Rah catches my eye through the reflection and gives me a look as if to say it's time to roll and I couldn't agree with him more. We've both had enough drama for one day.

"Did you hear what I just said?" Nellie says, stepping up to Nigel as Mickey rises from the futon and steps up to her. "You may not be the father of Mickey's baby." As the words sink in, Mickey looks from Nigel to Nellie, waiting for the next move. Chance, Rah, and I wait in silence.

"What happens between me and Mickey is between me and Mickey," Nigel says, throwing another basket. Mickey returns to her seat and Rah and I get up to leave. Nellie looks around the room and feels humiliated. I told her this would happen. She runs past us to go outside and Chance is right behind her.

"Man, I've got to pick up my brother. I'll holla at you later," Rah says. "Jayd, you ready?"

"Yeah. See y'all at school tomorrow."

As we walk out of the house I can see Nellie and Chance talking in his car. I know there's going to be some drama to follow in the morning. I know she thinks she was trying to help but that's the problem with giving people things they don't want: they have the right to throw it back in your face, no matter if they needed it or not.

START YOUR OWN BOOK CLUB

Courtesy of the DRAMA HIGH series

ABOUT THIS GUIDE

The following is intended to help you get
the book club you've always wanted
up and running!
Enjoy!

Start Your Own Book Club

A book club is not only a great way to make friends, but it is also a fun and safe environment for you to express your views and opinions on everything from fashion to teen pregnancy. A teen book club can also become a forum or venue to air grievances and plan remedies for problems.

The People

To start, all you need is yourself and at least one other person. There're no criteria for who this person or persons should be other than their having a desire to read and a commitment to discuss things during a certain time frame.

The Rules

Just as in Jayd's life, sometimes even book club discussions can be filled with much drama. People tend to disagree with each other, cut each other off when speaking, and take criticism personally. So, there should be some ground rules:

1. Do not attack people for their ideas or opinions.
2. When you disagree with a book club member on a point, disagree respectfully. This means that you do not denigrate other people for their ideas or even the ideas themselves, i.e., no name-calling or saying, "That's stupid!" Instead, say, "I can respect your position, however, I feel differently."
3. Back up your opinions with concrete evidence, either from the book in question or life in general.
4. Allow everyone a turn to comment.
5. Do not cut-a member off when the person is speaking. Respectfully wait your turn.
6. Critique only the idea (and do so responsibly; saying "That's stupid!" is not allowed). Do not criticize the person.

7. Every member must agree to and abide by the ground rules.

Feel free to add any other ground rules you think might be necessary.

The Meeting Place

Once you've decided on members, and agreed to the ground rules, you should decide on a place to meet. This could be the local library, the school library, your favorite restaurant, a bookstore, or a member's home. Remember, though, if you decide to hold your sessions at a member's home, the location should rotate to another member's home for the next session. It's also polite for guests to bring treats when attending a book club meeting at a member's home. If you choose to hold your meetings in a public place, always remember to ask the permission of the librarian or store manager. If you decide to hold your meetings in a local bookstore, ask the manager to post a flyer in the window announcing the book club, to attract more members if you so desire.

Timing is Everything

Teenagers of today are all much busier than teenagers of the past. You're probably thinking, "Between chorus rehearsals, the drama club, and oh yeah, my job, when will I ever have time to read another book that doesn't feature Romeo and Juliet!" Well, there's always time, if it's time well-planned and time planned ahead. You and your book club can decide to meet as often or as little as is appropriate for your bustling schedules. *Once a month* is a favorite option. *Sleepover Book Club* meetings—if you're open to excluding one gender—is also a favorite option. And in this day of high-tech, savvy teens, *Internet Discussion Groups* are also an appealing option. Just choose what's right for you!

Well, you've got the people, the ground rules, the place, and the time. All you need now is a book!

The Book

Choosing a book is the most fun. COURTIN' JAYD is of course an excellent choice, and since it's part of a series, you won't soon run out of books to read and discuss. Your book club can also have comparative discussions as you compare the first book, THE FIGHT, with the second, SECOND CHANCE, and so on.

But depending upon your reading appetite, you may want to veer outside of the Drama High series. That's okay. There are plenty of options, many of which you will be able to find under the Dafina Books for Young Readers program in the coming months.

Don't be afraid to mix it up. Nonfiction is just as good as fiction and a fun way to learn about where we came from without just using a history textbook. Science fiction and fantasy can be fun, too!

And always, always research the author. You might find the author has a website where you can post your book club's questions or comments. The author may even have an e-mail address available so you can correspond directly. Authors might also sit in on your book club meetings, either in person, or on the phone, and this can be a fun way to discuss the book as well!

The Discussion

Every good book club discussion starts with questions. COURTIN' JAYD, as does every book in the Drama High series, comes with a Reading Group Guide for your convenience, though of course, it's fine to make up your own. Here are some sample questions to get started:

1. What's this book all about anyway?
2. Who are the characters? Do we like them? Do they remind us of real people?
3. Was the story interesting? Were real issues of concern to you examined?
4. Were there details that didn't quite work for you or ring true?
5. Did the author create a believable environment—one that you could visualize?
6. Was the ending satisfying?
7. Would you read another book from this author?

Record Keeper

It's generally a good idea to have someone keep track of the books you read. Often libraries and schools will hold reading drives where you're rewarded for having read a certain number of books in a certain time period. Perhaps a pizza party awaits!

Get Your Teachers and Parents Involved

Teachers and parents love it when kids get together and read. So involve your teachers and parents. Your book club may read a particular book whereby it would help to have an adult's perspective as part of the discussion. Teachers may also be able to include what you're doing as a book club in the classroom curriculum. That way, books you love to read, such as the Drama High ones, can find a place in your classroom alongside the books you don't love to read so much.

Resources

To find some new favorite writers, check out the following resources. Happy reading!

Young Adult Library Services Association
http://www.ala.org/ala/yalsa/yalsa.htm

Carnegie Library of Pittsburgh
Hip-Hop!
Teen Rap Titles
http://www.carnegielibrary.org/teens/read/booklists/teen rap.html

TeensPoint.org
What Teens Are Reading
http://www.teenspoint.org/reading_matters/book_list.asp?s ort=5&list=274

Teenreads.com
http://www.teenreads.com

Sacramento Public Library
Fantasy Reading for Kids
http://www.saclibrary.org/teens/fantasy.html

Book Divas
http://www.bookdivas.com

MegCabot.com
http://www.megcabot.com/

HAVEN'T HAD ENOUGH?
CHECK OUT THESE GREAT SERIES
FROM DAFINA BOOKS!

DRAMA HIGH
by L. Divine
Follow the adventures of a young sistah who's learning life in the hood is nothing compared to life in high school.

THE FIGHT	SECOND CHANCE	JAYD'S LEGACY
ISBN: 0-7582-1633-5	ISBN: 0-7582-1635-1	ISBN: 0-7582-1637-8

FRENEMIES	LADY J	COURTIN' JAYD
ISBN: 0-7582-2532-6	ISBN: 0-7582-2534-2	ISBN: 0-7582-2536-9

BOY SHOPPING
by Nia Stephens
An exciting "you pick the ending" series that lets the reader pick Mr. Right.

BOY SHOPPING	LIKE THIS AND LIKE THAT	GET MORE
ISBN: 0-7582-1929-6	ISBN: 0-7582-1931-8	ISBN:0-7582-1933-4

DEL RIO BAY CLIQUE
by Paula Chase
A wickedly funny series that explores friendship, betrayal, and how far some people will go for popularity.

SO NOT THE DRAMA	DON'T GET IT TWISTED
ISBN: 0-7582-1859-1	ISBN: 0-7582-1861-3

PERRY SKKY JR.
by Stephanie Perry Moore
An inspirational series that follows the adventures of a high school football star as he balances faith and the temptations of teen life.

PRIME CHOICE	PRESSING HARD
ISBN: 0-7582-1863-X	ISBN: 0-7582-1872-9

PROBLEM SOLVED	PRAYED UP
ISBN: 0-7582-1874-5	ISBN: 0-7582-2538-5